Todd propped his elbows on his knees and rested his forehead in his hands. "I wasn't sure you'd be here," he mumbled, staring at his own feet.

"Of course I'd be here. Gin-Yung was my friend."

When Elizabeth reached again for his hand, Todd looked around almost guiltily.

"I'm only trying to comfort you, Todd." Suddenly she wondered if he thought Gin-Yung's ghost was watching from the next world. Even if it was true, she wouldn't have minded their holding hands. Gin-Yung had wanted Todd to love—and be loved—after she was gone. Right now Elizabeth knew Todd needed someone to help take away the pain of losing her.

"Liz, I'm so . . . I just can't—"

"Shhh." She pulled him close. "I'm here."

Todd laid his head against Elizabeth's shoulder, but he felt stiff in her arms, as if he was uncomfortable with her touch. *No, that's just my imagination,* she assured herself. *He's hurting.* She rested her hand against his thick, sandy hair. The familiar scent of his shampoo and aftershave reminded her of the nights they'd spent at Miller's Point when they were in high school. Gently, before she realized what she was doing, Elizabeth caressed the smooth skin at the back of his neck.

He moaned softly and pulled away. "Don't."

Bantam Books in the Sweet Valley University series.
Ask your bookseller for the books you have missed.

And don't miss these Sweet Valley
University Thriller Editions:

Visit the Official Sweet Valley Web Site on the Internet at:

http://www.sweetvalley.com

SWEET VALLEY UNIVERSITY®

Out of the Picture

Written by
Laurie John

Created by
FRANCINE PASCAL

BANTAM BOOKS
NEW YORK · TORONTO · LONDON · SYDNEY · AUCKLAND

RL 6, age 12 and up

OUT OF THE PICTURE

A Bantam Book / October 1997

Sweet Valley High® *and Sweet Valley University*®
are registered trademarks of Francine Pascal.
Conceived by Francine Pascal.
Produced by Daniel Weiss Associates, Inc.
33 West 17th Street
New York, NY 10011.

ISBN: 0-553-57057-9

Published simultaneously in the United States and Canada

Bantam Books are published by Bantam Books, a division of Bantam
Doubleday Dell Publishing Group, Inc. Its trademark, consisting of the
words "Bantam Books" and the portrayal of a rooster, is Registered in
U.S. Patent and Trademark Office and in other countries. Marca
Registrada. Bantam Books, 1540 Broadway, New York, New York 10036.

PRINTED IN THE UNITED STATES OF AMERICA

OPM   0 9 8 7 6 5 4 3 2 1

To Edward Hoagland

Chapter One

"Excuse me," Elizabeth Wakefield whispered as she edged past a dark-suited, somber-faced man. As organ music swelled, indicating the end of Gin-Yung Suh's funeral service, Elizabeth slipped out the heavy double doors and sank down onto the nearest concrete bench. She sighed with relief to be out in the clean, crisp morning air; inside, she thought she'd suffocate. Not that the Everlasting Peace Funeral Home wasn't lovely—it was, but the overpowering smell of flowers and the overwhelming sadness of the mourners had become too much for her.

Looking out across the beautifully manicured lawn, Elizabeth shivered. She could feel the conflicting sensations of the coolness of the concrete bench through her black skirt and the warmth of the sun through her black silk jacket. Her emotions seemed to be following the same zigzagging,

1

hot-cold pattern. She couldn't concentrate on any one thought for more than a moment.

A breeze swept past, causing a few strands of hair to come loose from Elizabeth's French twist. She brushed them out of her face and looked into the cloudless blue sky. Even though the day had turned out to be slightly cooler than normal for southern California, it was still perfectly beautiful. Just the kind of day Gin-Yung would have loved.

"I wish you were here with me now, Gin-Yung," Elizabeth murmured, dabbing at her eyes with a soggy tissue. "I wish you could feel this warm sunlight and see this gorgeous day. I . . . I can't believe you're *gone!*"

Elizabeth shook her head in amazement. Because Gin-Yung had kept her illness so well hidden, it seemed almost as if the brain tumor had claimed her life overnight.

It isn't fair, she thought. *It just isn't fair. You were so young, so funny, so full of life, Gin. And now you're gone.*

Elizabeth laid her hand against the smooth concrete bench. Was it really a week since she'd seen Gin-Yung sitting on a similar bench in the Sweet Valley University quad? Closing her eyes, she could still picture the way Gin-Yung had looked, sitting there with the sunlight glinting off her glossy, blue-black hair. At the time Elizabeth hadn't even known it was her; in fact, no one had known that Gin-Yung had come home from her internship in London.

2

And I was upset when I found out, Elizabeth reminded herself guiltily, remembering how she had gotten back together with her high-school boyfriend, Todd Wilkins, while Gin-Yung, his then-girlfriend, was overseas. When she discovered that Gin-Yung had returned to Sweet Valley, the only thing Elizabeth cared about was how it would affect her and Todd. She didn't take the time to seek Gin-Yung out . . . didn't even know she was dying until it was almost too late.

"I'm so sorry, Gin-Yung," Elizabeth whispered. "I wish I could take everything back. I'd do it all differently."

More organ music floated through the fragrant air as the double doors opened behind her and a handful of football players walked out, passing Elizabeth without a glance. The funeral home had been packed with SVU jocks who had known Gin-Yung through her job as a sports reporter for the *Sweet Valley Gazette*. The place had been jammed wall-to-wall with family members, college friends, fellow reporters, professors. . . . It seemed almost as if all of Sweet Valley had turned out for the service.

Elizabeth was digging in her purse for another tissue when she felt a gentle hand on her shoulder.

"Are you OK?" Nina Harper asked, sitting beside her and giving her a reassuring hug.

"I think so," Elizabeth replied, sniffling.

"I got a little worried when you bailed out early."

3

"Just needed some fresh air." Elizabeth sighed. "Nina . . . thanks for coming with me this morning."

"Hey, what are best friends for?" Nina handed her a fresh tissue. "Gin-Yung is . . . *was* a special person. And there's no way I'd have let you come here all by yourself." Her comforting gaze suddenly turned cloudy. "Since Todd couldn't—"

Elizabeth held up her hand and shook her head vigorously. She'd already explained why she hadn't come to the funeral with Todd. The last thing she wanted was to go into it again. For most of the day Elizabeth had been trying not to think about Todd—and failing miserably. She had hardly taken her eyes off him through the entire service.

"Everyone is paying their last respects to Gin-Yung's family," Nina pointed out. "Do you want to get in line? I'll stand with you."

"Thanks, Nina, but . . ." Elizabeth took a deep breath, trying to compose herself. But it was no use; her emotions were gaining enough speed and intensity to crush her. Her lower lip quivered uncontrollably. "I . . . I don't think I can h-handle that right n-now." Tears began to roll mercilessly down Elizabeth's cheeks. She wiped them away with trembling fingers.

Nina's deep brown eyes shone in sympathy. She dug in her purse and passed Elizabeth a second fresh tissue.

"They hate me." Elizabeth sniffed loudly and

4

coughed. "The Suhs must really hate me."

"Don't be ridiculous," Nina whispered, glancing over her shoulder at the mob of strangers who were now pouring out the double doors. "C'mon. Let's move someplace a little more out of the way."

Elizabeth let Nina take her arm and lead her to a shady spot beneath a sprawling oak tree. "Gin-Yung's family doesn't hate you," Nina said sternly. "You've got to get over that idea."

"They do, Nina. They hate me for taking Todd away from Gin-Yung. She was dying, and I stole her boyfriend!"

"You *didn't* steal—"

"You should've seen their faces at the hospital, Nina. You should've seen the way they kept *staring* at me. Especially Gin's big sister, Kim-Mi. I *know* she hates me. She probably wishes *I* had died instead of—"

"Stop it!" Nina gripped Elizabeth's shoulders. "Liz, what you saw on their faces was worry and sadness, not hate. Look, I *know* you. You're just overreacting because you're feeling guilty."

Elizabeth gulped. "Maybe . . . but I still can't face them right now."

"It's OK. You don't have to." Nina released her. "I doubt they're going to remember much about today anyway. They all look like they're in a state of shock."

"Of course they are. This whole thing is so unreal. Gin-Yung was barely nineteen years old, Nina.

5

I can't even imagine what her family must be going through."

And Todd, she thought guiltily. *Poor, poor Todd—his heart must be breaking!*

"Me either," Nina said, biting her bottom lip. "It must be the worst feeling in the world for a parent to lose a child. Seeing Gin-Yung's mother crying in there made me think about my own mom. You know how possessive she is. Remember how crazy she was about my coming to SVU in the first place? She couldn't even bear to let me out of her sight for a month at a time. Think how she'd feel if she knew she'd never see me again!"

"I know," Elizabeth said absently. She was trying to listen to her friend, but now her addled brain had flip-flopped back to thinking about Todd, which it always seemed to do lately, no matter how hard she tried to stop it.

I should be with him now, she thought. *I should be comforting him.*

"Can you believe how many people are here?" Nina exclaimed. "Everyone we know."

Everyone but Tom Watts, Elizabeth thought. She'd scanned the crowd several times, looking for him. Not that she'd wanted to see him, of course, but she had at least expected him to be there. She was already painfully aware of how uncaring her ex-boyfriend could be, but she couldn't believe he could be so callous and unfeeling as to not show up for the funeral of a friend. Suddenly she felt

6

ashamed for even thinking of him at all.

"There's Danny and Isabella. I'm surprised Tom's not with them, aren't you?" Nina asked, as if she'd read Elizabeth's mind. Danny Wyatt was Tom's roommate and best friend. He was a great guy, but Elizabeth hadn't seen that much of him since she and Tom had broken up.

As Danny and Isabella Ricci passed, arm in arm, they smiled slightly and said hello but didn't stop to talk. Maybe Nina was right. Maybe her guilty feelings were making her feel paranoid. It seemed to Elizabeth that Danny and Isabella had given her weird looks.

"Oh, here come Winston and Denise. Listen," Nina said, laying a hand on Elizabeth's arm. "If you don't mind, I'm going to ask them for a ride back to campus. I have a twelve o'clock advanced chemistry class that I really don't need to miss."

Elizabeth nodded. She was well aware that Nina was almost as fanatical about attending classes and getting her work done as she was, but Elizabeth was sure that Nina was merely using the class as an excuse to leave Elizabeth alone to go to Todd.

Winston Egbert, usually the life of the party, was stony-faced as he hugged Elizabeth. The same was true for his girlfriend, Denise Waters; her normally cheerful face was shrouded in sorrow.

"Todd should be out soon," Winston whispered. "He's still with Gin-Yung's family."

"I know," Elizabeth said, giving Winston a reassuring smile despite her own misery.

It must be so awkward for all my friends, she realized, *knowing that Todd left me to be at Gin-Yung's side while she was dying.*

"Winnie." Denise tapped him on the shoulder. "Is it OK for Nina to catch a ride back to campus with us?"

"Sure, no problem. We'll leave as soon as Maia comes out. She's riding with us too."

"Are you sure you'll have room for me?" Nina asked.

Winston grinned and looked more like his usual self. "In the sumptuous orange Bug we'll have room to spare."

While they waited for Maia Stillwater, Alexandra Rollins and her boyfriend, Noah Pearson, walked up. Alex looked as if she were about to hug Elizabeth, but then she stopped.

"How are you, Elizabeth? I haven't seen you in quite a while," Alex said.

"I'm fine, Alex." Enid Rollins, or Alex, as she now called herself, had been Elizabeth's best friend back at Sweet Valley High, but high school seemed so long ago, and so much had changed. She and Alex rarely did more than say a passing hello to each other anymore. Elizabeth missed her old friend, but she knew that things between them would never be the same as they were in high school.

"I'd heard you and Todd were back together," Alex said almost timidly.

Elizabeth didn't know how to take the comment—or quite how to answer. It was true that she and Todd had gotten back together when Gin-Yung was away in London. They'd had a wonderful, magical time that Elizabeth fully expected to last forever, but it had come to a crashing halt last week when Gin-Yung went into the hospital. Learning the seriousness of Gin-Yung's illness, they'd decided that Todd should be at her side.

Despite her own loneliness, Elizabeth knew Todd had done the right thing. And besides, Elizabeth couldn't have loved him if he hadn't been a person who cared about loyalty and compassion. But his involvement with the Suh family now seemed so complete, Elizabeth wasn't so sure herself if they would get back together or not.

The crowd on the lawn had grown so thick that Elizabeth could no longer see who was coming out of the funeral home. She craned her neck, afraid that she would miss Todd. But she needn't have worried; when the Suh family emerged, the crowd parted to let them down the sidewalk. Todd shuffled along with them, staring at the ground. His sandy brown hair and tall frame made him extremely conspicuous amid the raven-haired Suhs.

Elizabeth watched as Todd lifted his bowed head to speak to Kim-Mi Suh. His eyes were rimmed with red, and he looked pale and tired. Kim-Mi patted Todd's shoulder, then they gave each other a consoling hug.

"He looks awful," Alex whispered in Elizabeth's ear. "I know he really must have loved her. Did you notice how he broke down when they closed the casket and laid the roses on top?"

Elizabeth simply nodded. She didn't trust her voice to speak.

Noah's eyes began to water. Elizabeth, remembering how Noah and Gin-Yung had become good friends during their cruise on the SS *Homecoming Queen,* wished she could comfort him. Instead her own tears started to fall again.

"Let's go, Winnie," Denise whispered.

"All right, but we should say something to Todd first."

As the Suhs made their way toward the waiting limousines, Todd was left alone on the sidewalk. Instantly his friends filled in around him, shoving Elizabeth forward in the process.

"We're sorry, Todd," Winston said, clamping a hand on Todd's shoulder. "We feel for you, man."

"Is there anything we can do?" Denise asked.

Alex pushed forward and gave Todd a sisterly hug. "Hang in there, Todd. Call me if you need to talk."

"We know you're going to miss her," Noah said.

"We'll all miss her, Todd," said Maia, the Oakley Hall resident assistant.

Everyone was talking at once. Todd looked up as if searching for a life raft in the sea of well-meaning friends. When his eyes met Elizabeth's, her breath caught in her throat. She could tell he was struggling to keep his emotions under control, but he appeared to be losing the battle. Suddenly he pushed his way through the crowd and hurried off.

Elizabeth ran after him.

Jessica Wakefield paused on the steps outside the funeral home, squinting in the sudden bright sunlight until she could adjust the wide brim of her stylish black hat to shade her eyes. She frowned slightly at the sight of Elizabeth, her identical twin sister, chasing Todd Wilkins into the formal garden. *Elizabeth and her boyfriends!* she thought. *Usually I'm the one with the boyfriend troubles, but that's a thing of the past now that I've found the perfect man.*

She glanced over her shoulder at her boyfriend, Nick Fox. Just the sight of him made her feel all melty inside. He always looked sexy in the casual clothes he wore as an undercover cop, but today, dressed in a perfectly tailored dark suit and tie, he was positively heart stopping.

She felt the comforting warmth of his hand at her waist as they walked down the marble steps and into the crowd that had gathered on the lawn.

"Oh, Nick. This whole thing doesn't seem

real." She stepped back and looked into Nick's jade green eyes. "I just saw Gin-Yung last week, and she looked perfectly fine." She didn't bother explaining that at the time, she had nearly attacked the poor girl. Jessica had cornered her in Waggoner Hall and accused her of coming back from London just to steal Todd back from Elizabeth.

Nick wrapped his arms around her in a reassuring hug and touched his lips to her forehead. "Sometimes that's the way it happens," he said. "One day someone's here, and the next . . ."

Jessica's mind wandered back to that day in Waggoner Hall. *How was I supposed to know Gin-Yung was dying? And anyway, why should I feel guilty? I did it for Liz. I wouldn't get myself into these situations if my sugar sweet twin wasn't such a doormat.*

"Gin-Yung was such a sweet person," Jessica said, conveniently clearing her guilt from her mind. "We're all going to miss her. Especially Todd and Elizabeth."

Nick took Jessica's hand and held it in both of his. "I was really touched when her little sister, Chung-Hee, stood up and read that poem Gin-Yung had written."

"It *was* a beautiful ceremony," Jessica agreed tearily. "The kind of thing that really makes you think."

"What about?"

"You know. *Life*." She pulled her hand away from Nick's and used it to gesture grandly. "Gin-Yung's funeral made me realize how fleeting it can be. One minute you have it, and then *poof,* it's gone." Jessica snapped her fingers for emphasis. "It's wrong how people take their time on earth for granted. Life is too important to waste. It's just too bad that it takes something like this to re-mind us that we need to squeeze every ounce of excitement, fun, and adventure out of every single second."

Nick captured her gesturing hand long enough to kiss it. "I can't imagine *you* need to be re-minded of that."

"*Everybody* needs to be reminded of that!" Jessica tugged at the hem of her short black skirt. "This experience has really opened my eyes. I in-tend to turn over a new leaf—really reach out for life," she said dramatically. "After today I'm deter-mined to never let my life get boring."

Nick covered his mouth with his hand to hide his smile. He leaned so close, she could smell his spicy aftershave. "No danger of that, Jess. Life is never boring when you're around."

"You know what I mean, Nick. I want to really live life to the fullest."

"How could your life be any fuller when you have me?" he teased, striking a tough-guy pose.

She stifled a giggle. How could she argue with that? She wrapped her arms around Nick's muscular

13

chest and pressed her face against it. As she slid her hand along his back in a gentle caress, her fingers accidentally brushed against the gun that was tucked into his waistband at the small of his back. A shiver of excitement skittered up her spine. She pulled away from the hug and looked at his smug grin, which reminded her where she was going with this conversation in the first place.

Why is Nick pretending to be so thickheaded? she wondered. *He knows what I'm talking about. Our relationship is wonderful, but I want more. I want danger. Adrenaline-pumping action. Nonstop thrills. I want to be in on the things he takes for granted every day of his life.*

Jessica had already asked Nick to let her work with him undercover so many times, she didn't dare bring it up again—not directly. But why couldn't he take a hint? If he would just forgive and forget about the couple of times she'd scammed her way onto the scene of a bust or two, he might be more reasonable. It wasn't *her* fault things didn't go exactly as planned.

"Be serious," she said, running a finger across his chest. "I'm not talking about love. My life *is* full that way. I'm talking about excitement—the kind of stuff that makes your heart beat fast."

"You always make my heart beat fast."

"Nick!" She was beginning to get frustrated. This conversation was not going the way she wanted it to at all. "I don't know how you put up

14

with me," she began, taking another tack. "After all the exciting people you work with, I must seem pretty dull."

"Honey, nobody I work with is anywhere near as exciting as you are."

"Yeah, right. My life is so exciting . . . and dangerous!" She rolled her eyes. "Only this very morning I got my eyelashes caught in that little curler thingy—pulled three eyelashes out." Her bottom lip quivered slightly into a pout.

"Jessica, I know what you're trying to do."

"Oh, Nick, if I had an exciting job like yours—"

He shook his head violently. "No way. Absolutely not. And I don't want to talk about this again." He crossed his arms defiantly. "One cop in a relationship is plenty."

She stamped the ground and let out a huff. Why did he keep denying her the one thing she really wanted? Couldn't he see how much she needed to be a part of his life—*every* part of his life?

"Quit pouting. It's not going to work," he said firmly.

"But *Ni*-ick . . ." She laid her most beguiling expression on him.

"You drive me crazy sometimes, you know that?" His harsh expression relaxed, and his voice softened. For a moment she thought he was going to give in, but then he set his chiseled jaw and looked around at the crowd. "Maybe we'd better go see if your sister needs a ride back to campus," he suggested. "She looked pretty upset during the service."

Jessica scowled. Nick was *definitely* trying to ignore her if he had to resort to Elizabeth as a topic of conversation. Disappointed, she let him take her hand and lead her back toward the others.

"Do you see her?" he asked.

"Liz? She's around here somewhere. I saw her chasing Todd into the bushes a few minutes ago."

"Don't you think you should check on her?"

"Elizabeth can take care of herself."

He pulled her close and brushed her cheek with his hand. "Just because you're mad at *me* for putting an end to our little talk doesn't mean you should take it out on your own twin."

"I'm not!" Jessica insisted. "Besides, who said our 'little talk' was over? As far as I'm concerned, it's just postponed."

Nick sighed. "Why don't I go get the car and you go find Elizabeth? You two can meet me down at the edge of the sidewalk."

Huffily Jessica turned away and tossed her hair over her shoulder. Without another word, she began the search for Elizabeth.

"Todd," Elizabeth whispered hoarsely as she hurried along the flagstone garden path after him. Thinking he hadn't heard her, she called more loudly, "Todd, please wait."

16

At last he stopped and waited for her to catch up.

"Are you OK?" she asked. "I've been so worried about you."

When he didn't answer, Elizabeth reached for Todd's hand and entwined her fingers with his. She led him to a little white wrought iron bench that was nestled under an arched trellis covered with wild roses. She squeezed his hand consolingly, but he pulled it free before sitting down.

Todd propped his elbows on his knees and rested his forehead in his hands. "I wasn't sure you'd be here," he mumbled, staring at his own feet.

"Of course I'd be here. Gin-Yung was my friend."

"You understand why I sat with Gin-Yung's family today," he began. "I mean, you aren't upset about it, are you?"

"Not at all."

When Elizabeth reached again for his hand, Todd looked around almost guiltily.

"I'm only trying to comfort you, Todd." Suddenly she wondered if he thought Gin-Yung's ghost was watching from the next world. Even if it was true, she wouldn't have minded their holding hands. Gin-Yung was totally unselfish and giving. One of the last things she'd ever done was make up a story about having a new boyfriend in London so Todd and Elizabeth could be together without feeling guilty. Gin-Yung had wanted Todd

17

to love—and be loved—after she was gone. Right now Elizabeth knew Todd needed someone to help take the pain of losing her away.

"Liz, I'm so . . . I just can't—"

"Shhh." She pulled him close. "I'm here."

Todd laid his head against Elizabeth's shoulder, but he felt stiff in her arms, as if he was uncomfortable with her touch. *No, that's just my imagination,* she assured herself. *He's hurting.* She rested her hand against his thick, sandy hair. The familiar scent of his shampoo and aftershave reminded her of the nights they'd spent at Miller's Point when they were in high school. Gently, before she realized what she was doing, Elizabeth caressed the smooth skin at the back of his neck.

He moaned softly and pulled away. "Don't." A tear rolled down his cheek. "Elizabeth, I can't believe I'm saying this, but . . . I—I don't think we should keep seeing each other."

Elizabeth's eyes widened in shock. "You mean for a while? I know you need time," she said softly, wondering why he had to bring up their relationship at a time like this. "It's all right, Todd. I'm not going to rush you."

"No. That's not it." He bit his bottom lip and dropped his gaze to the ground. "This is so hard! I don't want to hurt you, Liz. I want you to try and understand what I'm about to say. I've been thinking about it and thinking about it . . . and

I've decided it's best that we just go our own ways now. End it."

The words hit her ears but hardly registered. "Are you saying you don't love me?"

"No. Of course not, but . . . well . . . I don't know, Elizabeth. It's not that I don't love you. It's more that I don't feel anything—for anybody. At the moment I just feel empty. It's . . . it's like my heart had this place for you and this place for Gin-Yung. Then when she died, it left this empty space like a vacuum that just sucked the whole thing in. This past week has been way too confusing. I don't know how to describe it."

Elizabeth reached again for his hand. He didn't pull away. "It's OK. This has been a confusing time for both of us. I understand."

"How? How can you understand, Liz, when I don't? I feel so guilty. I feel like I've let you both down. If I'd been a better boyfriend, maybe Gin-Yung would have come home sooner. Maybe she would have confided in me. Maybe I could have made a difference, you know?" He paused as tears fell from his eyes. "If I'd helped her cope with this thing, maybe she could have beat it somehow."

"Oh, Todd, you know better than that. The doctors in England told Gin-Yung the tumor was fatal before she ever came home."

Todd pulled away from Elizabeth's embrace, got up from the bench, and began to pick nervously at

19

a branch of the rosebush dangling between them like a thorny wall.

"And I let you down too," Todd continued as if he wanted to ignore her statement. "I'm so sorry. I never wanted to hurt you. When I told you that I didn't love Gin-Yung anymore, I really believed it. It was only after I realized I was losing her that I knew I'd been kidding myself. It's that old cliché about not knowing how much something means to you until you lose it."

"Todd—"

"I know now that I was just annoyed that Gin could so easily waltz off to London and leave me here alone. And now I finally realize how good I had it. I only wish she was still in London. At least I could call her and . . ." His voice cracked. "I should have been with her from the moment she came home. I know you're right, Liz . . . I couldn't have made any difference about her tumor. But I could have been more supportive. I should have been sharing her pain, giving her courage. Instead I was—"

"With me?" Elizabeth finished for him.

Todd broke off the rose he'd been twisting. He looked into Elizabeth's eyes until he seemed to regain control of himself. He sat back down on the bench beside her and handed her the crumpled rose. "Yes. I was with you, Elizabeth, but I don't regret being with you. Not for a second. I hope I haven't made it sound that way. Like I said, I'm all confused. But I'm glad we had that time together. When we broke up—you know, before . . ."

Elizabeth didn't want to wade back through the emotions of their horrible first weeks at SVU. "We worked all that out, remember? Going from high school to college presented a lot of changes for both of us. If we hadn't been under so much stress—"

"No, it was me. We both know it was my fault. I was the one causing the pressure—for you anyway. I was wrong to expect you to make love after you'd told me you weren't ready. . . . But that's not what I'm getting at."

Elizabeth stared up at him expectantly.

"What I'm trying to say is that when we broke up, all the wonderful times we'd shared through high school were wiped out by our anger and hurt. Getting back together was the best thing for both of us. It gave us a chance to recapture a lot of the old feelings. It gave us a chance to remember and to forgive."

Elizabeth wrapped her arms around him, wanting to let him know how much that time meant to her. Todd didn't pull away, but she could almost feel him slipping through her fingers.

"You do forgive me, don't you, Elizabeth?" His voice was muffled against her hair.

"You know I do, Todd."

"Now if I can only forgive myself."

"You'll have to," she said, sniffling.

21

"It won't be easy, but yeah, I'll have to. And I think I need to be alone until I can do that. I kept thinking during Gin's funeral about how things have to end. So maybe today is my day of closure—all around. For me and Gin, for you and me . . ."

Todd fixed his stare on the angel statue as tears ran down his face. For a few moments neither of them said a word. "So let's just make a clean break, OK?" Todd said, shattering the silence.

"OK, Todd, if that's what you want." She tossed the crumpled rose behind the bench. "So . . . it's over."

"Yes," he whispered. "But this time it's over without anger. I know you were the best thing that ever happened to me, but it's the past. You know what I mean? It's like we were both trying to go back to high school, where we were safe."

Although his words hurt, they seemed right somehow. Todd always had been her port in a storm, but she'd never meant to take advantage of him. "I guess you're right, but . . ." She bit her bottom lip to keep her tears from flowing. Todd had been a part of her life for almost as far back as she could remember. How was she supposed to just walk away now?

"I may be right," Todd began, "but I'm not a bit happy about it. I hope you know that."

"I do," Elizabeth replied, her heart clenching painfully. "I'll always love you, Todd. I can't help it. You're a part of me." She placed her palm against his warm, damp cheek. He pulled it away, but softly kissed her wrist before letting her go.

"And I'll never stop adoring you, Elizabeth. You'll always be my first love. No one can ever take that away from us."

They shared another warm hug, and Todd kissed Elizabeth's cheek. "If you don't mind, I need a little time alone before going to Gin-Yung's—I mean, the Suhs'."

Elizabeth squeezed his hands and smiled, or tried to smile. She wasn't sure if she succeeded or not. "I—" She swallowed back the "I love you" that had risen to her lips again. "I'll always be here for you, Todd," she said instead. "You know, when you need a friend." Her voice trembled, and her tears were about to betray her.

"I'll see you there later, OK?" Todd moved away from her, heading farther into the shady garden.

"Later," she whispered. Her outstretched hand found only empty air. She turned away, not telling him that she couldn't go on to the Suhs'. Not now. Not ever. But she doubted that in his present state of mind Todd would notice her absence anyway.

Todd was right. He was her past. But where was her future?

Chapter
Two

This is ridiculous, Lila Fowler thought. *And em-barrassing. People have probably been looking at me and thinking, "Why is she bawling? She and Gin-Yung weren't that close!" And yet here I am, tears streaming down my face like a fool. My mascara has probably run down to my chin. My nose probably looks like Rudolph's, and I'll bet I don't have an ounce of lipstick left. All because of this stupid purse!* She whacked the black leather Doinel purse in her lap with her fist.

Gin-Yung's funeral ceremony had hardly started when Lila, feeling a little teary eyed, had instinctively reached into the purse for a tissue. But instead of a Kleenex she'd pulled out an antique lace handkerchief—the very same lace handkerchief that her mother-in-law had pressed into her hand at the funeral for Tisiano, her husband. Suddenly the purse had become a Pandora's box of memories.

25

It seemed like a lifetime ago, but it wasn't that long really—just since high-school graduation. On a trip to Europe she had met and fallen in love with Tisiano, the handsome young Count di Mondicci. In a matter of weeks she had married into one of the richest and most powerful families in Europe. It was like a fairy tale, but a short, sad fairy tale that had ended when Tisiano was killed in a Jet Ski accident.

Normally cool and collected, Lila lost emotional control as wave after wave of repressed memories washed over her. Tisiano's smile . . . his twinkling eyes . . . his strong tanned shoulders . . . his laughter . . . his daring . . . but most of all, his death.

Throughout the service for Gin-Yung, Lila shed genuine tears. But they were tears for Tisiano. Tears that seemed to bubble up from somewhere so deep inside her, she didn't know such a place of sorrow existed.

When the service had ended and everyone had begun filing toward the Suhs to pay their last respects, Lila had gently laid a hand on the arm of her boyfriend, Bruce Patman, to let him know she wanted to stay put.

Together they had sat quietly, heads bowed, not speaking for what seemed like an eternity.

"Lila," Bruce whispered softly in her ear at last, "are you ready to leave? We're the last ones here."

She sniffed and wiped her nose. "Sorry, Bruce,

but I just couldn't let everyone see me this way." After all, Lila had a reputation to uphold. She had been raised to believe that people of her class were above public displays of emotion. "I'm so embarrassed."

"Don't be," he said. "People expect a few tears on an occasion like this."

"Not from Lila Fowler."

"Yes, even from the perfect, cool, composed Lila Fowler." Bruce dabbed at the corner of his own moist eye with his knuckle. "It's always tragic when someone so young and full of promise dies. It doesn't seem fair somehow—it's like they never got a chance to really live."

Lila stared at the handkerchief she held clutched in her fist.

"You were thinking of *him*, weren't you?" Bruce said, tilting her face up to his.

She tried to pull away and hide her face, but Bruce held her chin firmly.

Lila stared into his dark blue eyes, so full of compassion. "I just started remembering things, and I couldn't stop," she said in a tight, strained voice as her tears threatened to erupt again.

He wrapped his arm around her and stroked the back of her hair with his hand. "It's OK, my love," he whispered. "Let it out. Cry if you need to."

"We . . . we were only together such a short time, and then—" She pressed her face against his shoulder.

"Shhh," he whispered against her hair. "You don't have to explain. I understand how you feel."

She almost said, "No, you don't," but then remembered that when they were in high school, Bruce's girlfriend, Regina Morrow, had died of a drug overdose. The memory made Lila cling to Bruce even tighter—as if he could fade away. "You do understand me," she said instead. "You understand me better than anyone."

"And I always will," he assured her tenderly.

Why shouldn't he, when we're so much alike? Lila wondered. *And not just because we're both good-looking and rich and grew up having everything we both wanted. It's deeper than that. Sometimes it's like we're the same person, with the same thoughts and dreams and goals.*

Sighing, Lila silently thanked whatever lucky forces had finally brought her and Bruce together. She pulled away and touched her fingertips to her puffy cheeks. "I must look like a raccoon."

Bruce tilted her face toward his again. Holding her chin firmly, he began to wipe the smeared mascara from her face with his own crisp, white monogrammed handkerchief. "There." He flashed his most charming smile. "Damage repaired. Perfection restored."

"Thank you." She sniffled.

"Shall we?" He stood and offered her his arm.

Satisfied with his assurance that she looked as beautiful as ever, she stood, slung her black Doinel

28

purse over her shoulder, and slipped her arm into the crook of his elbow. But as they emerged into the sunlight her confidence left her once again.

"Let's slip around the side of the building and avoid that mob," Bruce suggested.

Lila nodded gratefully. Yes, Bruce knew her better than anyone. They were meant to be together. It was fate. The only thing that surprised her was that it had taken them so long to find each other. Not physically, of course. They had known each other all their lives, but they'd never even considered dating until they were forced together after a plane crash in the mountains during their Christmas break. It was hard to believe that in high school they'd practically hated each other. Maybe they'd had some growing up to do. Well, whatever their past differences, Lila had no doubts about their love now.

"We both have our ghosts, don't we?" she asked as they reached the parking lot.

Bruce nodded. "But I know what we need to chase away the ghosts of loves past."

"What?"

"We're going to go home and rest." A strand of his thick, dark hair fell across his forehead as he bent down and opened the door of his black Porsche. "After that, we're going to head out to the Verona Springs Country Club. In fact, let's spend the next few days there and make use of that ultraexpensive membership you talked me into."

Lila took in a deep, cleansing breath. "Oh, yes, let's!" She suddenly felt as if she'd been sprung from a cage. "That's *exactly* what we need."

The Verona Springs Country Club was a different world. Besides being one of the most beautiful clubs Lila had ever seen, it was a place where the ordinary problems of the world didn't exist. No dull college classes, no tests, no sorority pettiness, no memories of death. From the first moment she had crossed through those guarded wrought iron gates into that private, perfect world of privilege and class, she knew she had to belong. Like being with Bruce Patman, it was her destiny.

As Lila reached for her seat belt her head was so full of thoughts about the Verona Springs Country Club that she didn't notice that Mama di Mondicci's antique handkerchief had fallen to the black asphalt of the parking lot just before Bruce slammed the door.

Nick watched as Jessica ran across the lawn toward the garden where her sister, Elizabeth, stood, looking utterly lost. They looked like two beautiful blond angels against the backdrop of trees and flowers. It never ceased to amaze him how identical they looked. They had the same golden hair, the same blue-green eyes, the same heart-melting smiles, the same adorable dimples in their left cheek, and even the same athletic yet willowy model's figure.

Still, no two girls could have been more different in personality.

And it's a good thing, Nick thought. *If they had the same personality, then I'd have a tough time choosing. Jessica Wakefield is spontaneous as a flash flood and twice as much trouble sometimes, but I love her more than anything.*

Nick agreed with Jessica's philosophy about funerals making you think. All morning Nick's thoughts had been drawn to Todd Wilkins. He felt so sorry for the guy. Nick knew that if he'd been in Todd's situation and had his girlfriend die right in his arms, he couldn't have coped half as well as Wilkins had. For a moment tears blurred his vision. He couldn't imagine what he'd do if he lost Jessica. The thought was simply unbearable.

His blood ran cold as he remembered that moment at the chop shop bust when Jessica had suddenly appeared from nowhere. All his years of police training had failed him the moment he knew that Jessica was in danger. Since joining the police force he had been held at gunpoint, been attacked by a knife-wielding, drug-crazed robber, and once even had gone over the edge of a bridge while trying to talk down an attempted suicide, but nothing had ever scared him as much as seeing Jessica in the line of fire. He never wanted to be in that situation again as long as he lived.

No, I couldn't stand to lose Jess. Not ever. That's why he'd ignored her hints about letting her come with him when he was on a case. The sooner she got that crazy idea out of her mind, the better. He would do anything to keep her out of danger.

He jogged across the busy street and headed toward the next block, where they'd had to park, thanks to Jessica's need to try on half her wardrobe before deciding on what to wear to the funeral.

I even love your lateness, Jessica Wakefield, he thought, smiling.

I wish I'd asked Nina to stay with me, Elizabeth thought miserably as she emerged from the garden. During the time she'd been with Todd, the crowd on the chapel lawn had dwindled to a handful of unfamiliar faces. Now she felt totally abandoned. But suddenly her spirits soared as she saw Jessica hurrying toward her.

Elizabeth ran to her sister's side and enveloped her in a hug. She was comforted by the thought that no matter how different they were or how much they disagreed, Jessica was always there for her when she needed her.

"Did I just see Nick leave?" Elizabeth asked with a sniff when they finally pulled apart.

"He's gone to get the car. There was such a crowd when we first got here that we had to park three blocks away. Isn't that awful? A place like this should really provide more parking." She rolled her eyes. "And *then,* on top of that, we had to stand at the back all during the funeral service. Can you believe it? These heels are killing me." Jessica looked down at her feet. "Oh, I borrowed your black heels, by the way. I knew you wouldn't mind. Where's Todd?"

"He's still in the garden," Elizabeth replied, momentarily bewildered by her sister's chatter.

Jessica's eyes widened. "All by himself?"

"He wanted to be alone."

"And you didn't argue?" Jessica pursed her lips disapprovingly.

"There was no reason to argue, Jess. It's over. Todd and I have decided to go our separate ways."

"Todd and you decided, or just Todd decided?"

"We both think it's best," Elizabeth murmured, looking away.

"Yeah, right. Who are you trying to convince— me or yourself?"

Elizabeth felt her eyes stinging with tears, but she blinked them back.

Jessica huffed indignantly. "I don't get it. It's not fair. You were back together, and everything was fine, and then just because of Gin-Yung—"

"No, it's not because of Gin-Yung . . . not really." Elizabeth shook her head. "We just weren't meant to be together, that's all."

Jessica narrowed her eyes and stared over Elizabeth's shoulder toward the garden. "Maybe I should have a little talk with young Mr. Wilkins," she snarled.

"Jessica, don't. Please. Todd has a lot on his mind right now."

"But—"

"Really. And don't look at me like that either," Elizabeth pleaded, noting the stern set of Jessica's jaw. "I'll be fine." She knew she wasn't fooling her sister by putting on a brave face, but she continued anyway. "It'll just take some getting used to, that's all."

"Jeez," Jessica grumbled, leaning on Elizabeth while she bent one leg, pulled off an offending shoe, and rubbed her toes. "How can you stand it, Liz? It seems like lately the people you depend on the most won't stick around. First Tom and now Todd—or maybe I should say, first Todd and then Tom, and now Todd again—"

Despite the pain she was feeling, Elizabeth had to smile at the simple way her sister summed up her college year. Only Jessica Wakefield could accurately measure time by boyfriends. "The important people stick around," she said.

"Like who?"

"Like you, Jess," Elizabeth said, supporting Jessica while she stepped back into her shoe. When Jessica was back on two feet, Elizabeth put an arm around her shoulders. "As long as I have you, I'll be fine. You'll never leave me, will you?"

"Oh, no problem there. You're stuck with me

forever. If I wasn't around, who'd put a little excitement in your life?"

"Who'd borrow my clothes, eat all my snacks, or hog the phone?"

"Or wreck the room or help you spend all that money you horde?"

"Or torment me about studying too much or working too hard?"

"Right. I'm pretty essential to your life, aren't I?" Jessica leaned toward her sister with a grin.

Elizabeth hugged her twin. "Yes, you are." As if she hadn't been crying enough all morning, tears of love and gratitude now rushed to her eyes.

"Here comes Nick," Jessica said as the black Camaro pulled up to the curb. They walked over to the side of the car as Nick climbed out.

"Elizabeth, can we drop you back at the dorm?" he asked, his cool green eyes soft with genuine concern.

"Thanks, Nick, but I have the Jeep."

"Are you sure you want to drive back alone? Jess could drive the Jeep and you could ride with me, or Jess could ride with you and—"

"No. I'll be OK." Elizabeth smiled at Nick. Rarely did she agree with Jessica's choice in men, but for once Jessica had picked a good guy. Nick was not only good-looking—that was a given for any guy Jessica dated—but he was honest and mature and extremely responsible. Exactly what Jessica needed.

"Are you sure?" he repeated, holding the car door open while Jessica slid inside.

She nodded. "I really would rather drive back alone, honestly. I need the time to think."

After giving Elizabeth a quick, awkward hug, Nick climbed into the car beside Jessica and started the engine. With a brief wave they roared away, leaving Elizabeth standing on the curb.

Elizabeth walked back to the parking lot, where her red Jeep and Todd's blue BMW were the last remaining cars.

Should I try again to comfort him? she wondered. She wanted to. Elizabeth was so drawn toward the garden, she felt as if some kind of invisible force were pulling her. *Maybe if I go to him now . . . no.* She stopped herself practically midstep. *Todd made it pretty clear he didn't want me around. I have to let him deal with this on his own.*

With tears in her eyes she blew a kiss toward the garden, where her first love still sat with his ghosts.

Completely exhausted from his morning run, Tom Watts stumbled into the lobby of Reid Hall. Even though his legs felt like rubber bands and his side ached, he paused long enough to peek through the tiny window of his mailbox. *Nothing!*

"You're living in a dream world, Watts," he muttered to himself in disappointment as he dragged himself up the stairs to his dorm room. Too tired to bother with the key, he raised his hand to knock. But then he remembered that his roommate, Danny Wyatt, wouldn't be there.

No wonder there's practically no one around, he reminded himself. *Everyone's at Gin-Yung's funeral—where I should be too, if I wasn't such a coward.* He fished in the pocket of his sweats for his key and tried to ignore the empty gnawing feeling in the pit of his stomach. He knew it wasn't hunger; it was guilt. He'd felt like a traitor to his friends all morning. *But how could I have gone to the funeral, knowing that Elizabeth would be there?*

He could just imagine what it'd be like. He'd be aching to hold her, and all the while he'd have to sit there helplessly and watch her comforting Todd Wilkins instead.

Beautiful, innocent Elizabeth Wakefield. The most wonderful person who'd ever come into his life was no longer his. All the time they'd shared—all the laughter and love was gone, and who did he have to blame for that fact but himself?

When she had confided to him that his long lost biological father, George Conroy, was coming on to her, he'd accused her of trying to destroy his new family. But Tom was the one who'd done the destroying. By the time he'd found out that Elizabeth was telling the truth, he'd wrecked the strongest relationship he'd ever had. Thanks to his stupidity and temper, he'd driven Elizabeth right back into the arms of her first love—Todd Wilkins, superjock.

But he'd tried to make amends. He'd written Elizabeth a beautiful letter of apology. In that letter he'd flat-out admitted that everything was his fault. He'd told her that he was miserable without her and that he was a fool for taking his father's word over hers. He'd put as much work into that letter as he had into many stories he'd worked on at WSVU, the campus TV station, but so far she hadn't responded in any way. Maybe Danny was right. Maybe writing a letter *was* the cowardly way out. In any case, it hadn't worked.

Why, Elizabeth? he wondered. *I know you read it. Why are you ignoring me?*

Too afraid to face her in person, he'd left the letter on her desk at work. He could still remember how his heart had pounded the moment he'd noticed the letter was gone. Just the thought that she was reading his plea of forgiveness both terrified and excited him. He was terrified that she might throw the letter in his face and tell him to get lost, and he was excited to think that there might be a slim chance she would find it in her heart to forgive him. Even if she couldn't reply in person, he thought she would have called or written back by now.

Tom peeled off his sweaty T-shirt and tossed it over the back of his desk chair. He was about to head for the shower room when he noticed the stack of mail lying on his desk. *Danny must have picked up the mail before leaving for the funeral,* he thought as renewed hope swelled in his heart.

With trembling hands Tom snatched up the mail. He absently tossed aside the pizza coupons from Pizza Paradiso and the envelope that was obviously a bill from the campus bookstore. Coming to the last letter, he held his breath until he saw that it was official stationery from George Conroy's office. Then he let all his breath out at once in a noisy half cough, half snort.

Disgusted, he dropped the envelope back on the desk. What could George Conroy have to say that would interest him? Nothing! He could never forgive his father for ruining his life with Elizabeth—maybe forever. Mr. Conroy was a lecherous old liar. *No wonder my mother ordered the creep out of my life before I was born. He was probably chasing blond teenagers back then.*

But as guilty as his father was, Tom considered himself to be more so. He should never have taken Mr. Conroy's word over Elizabeth's. She had never lied to him before—so why did he suddenly believe she would lie about the time his father tried to kiss her? Why had he so stubbornly clung to the belief that his father was innocent before he saw the evidence with his own two eyes?

Tom shuddered as he remembered the stash of candid photos he'd found in his father's desk—

photos that proved beyond any doubt that Mr. Conroy had been following Elizabeth for weeks, taking pictures of her like some crazed stalker.

Even when Tom had confronted his father with the photos, the best excuse he could come up with was "sometimes things just happen that we have no control over." How lame!

He picked up the letter and aimed for the wastebasket, but a sudden thought stopped him from sending the missile into the trash. *What if this was Elizabeth's reaction when she found my letter on her desk? What if she threw away my hard-thought-out words without even looking at them?* Although he knew it had no effect whatsoever on what Elizabeth did or didn't do, some perverse sense of logic made him rip the envelope open.

Dear Son,

I know you don't want me to call you son, but I feel I have that right at last. Not just because I'm your biological father, but because of the closeness that developed between us since I found you. I waited twenty-one years to meet you. I cannot lose you now. I hope that you will eventually find it in your heart to forgive me.

Tom skimmed down the rest of the page. How could he forgive his father when he'd ruined the most important relationship of Tom's life?

Enclosed are two memberships to the Verona Springs Country Club. Please accept them as a gesture of my goodwill.

"Great," Tom muttered. "Now he's trying to *buy* me back." He unfolded the elaborately printed membership applications. *This must have set him back a bundle,* Tom realized. *But what's money to George? He has more than he and his two kids can ever spend.*

Tom rotated his neck, which was becoming stiffer by the second. *Anyway, he's already given me a trust fund that's made me financially secure for the first time in my life. Why would he think he could buy me with a club membership?*

Tom turned back to the letter.

Perhaps you could give the blank membership to Elizabeth.

With a harsh laugh Tom tossed the letter to his desk. "So *that's* it! You're not trying to buy back my love . . . you're trying to bring Elizabeth back into your clutches!" He snorted derisively. "Well, that just shows how little you know her, George. High society has never impressed Elizabeth. She would never even *visit* a place like that, much less become a member."

My first instincts were right, he decided. *This is trash.* He scooped the letter up—memberships and all—and tossed it into the wastebasket. "Go to hell, George Conroy. I don't need you or your bribes. I don't need anybody."

He stomped across the room and jerked open his top bureau drawer to get a clean T-shirt. There lay Elizabeth's framed picture, where he'd hidden it from Danny's prying eyes. She seemed to smile up at him in that patient, understanding way she had.

He laid his finger against the cool glass over her lips. What wouldn't he give to touch those lips for real again? To see the twinkle in those aqua eyes? To make that dimple appear in her left cheek? "I said I was sorry, Liz. What more can I do?" He leaned heavily against the bureau. His stomach was still aching, and now his legs seemed to no longer want to support him. "Who am I trying to kid," he moaned. "I *do* need someone. I need you, Elizabeth Wakefield."

He shoved the picture of Elizabeth beneath a few clean shirts and slammed the bureau drawer shut. As much as he wanted to stare at the picture for the rest of the day, he didn't dare leave it out where Danny could start asking questions or say, "I told you so." Danny had always seen Elizabeth as the innocent victim of Tom's hair-trigger temper. And in this case Tom agreed.

"Elizabeth, please . . . at least answer my letter." He flopped down on his bed and covered his face with his arms. "Don't you know how miserable I am without you?"

Nick flicked off the radio and glanced sideways at Jessica. "OK, let's have it. What's up?" he asked as he threaded his Camaro skillfully through the midday traffic.

Jessica just shrugged and continued to stare out the passenger-side window.

He reached over and pried loose the hand Jessica held clenched in her lap. "Why so quiet? It's not like you."

"You know why, Nick."

Nick sighed and released her hand. "Jessica, stop playing games. Tell me what's bothering you."

"What we talked about before. I told you the conversation wasn't over."

With one hand on the wheel Nick used his free hand to jerk loose his tie and unbutton the top button of his dress shirt. "Not the I-wanna-be-a-cop thing."

Jessica huffed and flounced in the seat. "Nick, please. Just let me come along with you on your next job."

"No. Absolutely not. It's out of the question."

"Why?" she cried, crossing her arms across her chest. "Why can't I have some excitement in my life once in a while? I'm so *tired* of my dull existence."

Nick smiled patiently. Nothing about Jessica's life could even remotely be described as dull. Her impetuous, daring, impulsive nature seemed to get her into more jams than Lucy Ricardo in the old *I Love Lucy* sitcom.

"I'm sick of the same old school routine. All I ever do is go to boring classes, sit around drinking tea at the sorority house, go to the campus snack bar with friends who yak about stale gossip. I want *adventure*. I want to live every day to the fullest. I want to be on the cutting edge of excitement."

"No, you don't," he said with a laugh. "You don't want to be on the edge of anything. I know you, Jessica. You want to be right smack in the middle."

"All right, then. Let me be in the middle of it. That's what I'm trying to tell you. Let me be your partner, Nick. Take me along next time you have a stakeout."

"No, Jess. It's impossible."

Jessica's eyes flashed. "You don't understand how I feel. You're *sooo* lucky. With you, excitement is an everyday part of the job. You're so used to it, you take it for granted."

"Being a cop is *not* all fun and excitement."

"Ohhh nooo, of course it isn't," Jessica drawled sarcastically.

Nick glanced in the rearview mirror and changed lanes. "My job is like anyone else's. Sometimes it's tiring. Sometimes it's aggravating. And sometimes it's downright frustrating. It's anything but glamorous. I spend most of my time chasing down dead-end leads, doing senseless paperwork, getting more training, and taking orders from bosses. It's the real world, Jess. Not a TV show."

"I'm perfectly aware of all that." She tossed her head all-knowingly. "Every job has its drawbacks."

"But . . . ?"

"*But* not every job is as exciting as yours. Can't I just come with you on your next case?"

If Nick hadn't been driving, he'd have put both hands over his ears. It seemed as if his job was all she ever talked about anymore. And hearing her talk about it was only half the problem. He knew when Jessica talked about doing something, it rarely ended there. Jessica could be as tenacious as a pit bull.

"Jess, we've talked about this a hundred times."

"No, *we* haven't. Not really. I talk, and you just say no."

Nick lightly punched the steering wheel. "I can't let you come with me when I'm working. It's too dangerous."

"If it's too dangerous for me, then it's too dangerous for you."

"But I'm *trained*. I have experience. I know what I'm doing. And even so, you're right; it's still dangerous for me. But I accept those risks— for myself because it's my job. I couldn't accept them for you. I'd never forgive myself if anything happened to you. I care about you too much."

"I'm doing this for your own good, Jessica," Jessica mimicked in a parental tone. "Jeez, if I had a dollar for every time I've heard that, I'd be richer than Lila!"

Nick parked in the visitor's slot in front of Dickenson Hall and turned to face her squarely. "Let's not talk about this any more today, please."

"Fine!" Jessica opened the passenger-side door and slid her long, tanned legs from the car. "Oh, and you don't have to walk me up to my dorm room. I think even little ol' me can make it across this big dangerous parking lot all by myself."

"Wait. Don't—"

She slammed the door so hard, his teeth jarred.

Nick leaned his forehead against the cool glass of the window and watched her stomp toward the dorm. Even when she was furious, she was the most beautiful girl he'd ever seen. He loved the way her golden hair bounced when she walked. Whenever he heard the phrase 'as precious as gold,' he thought of her.

How can I make her understand? he wondered, pulling out of the parking lot. He knew she wouldn't drop it. What Jessica wanted, Jessica usually got—whether it was good for her or not.

"What am I going to do?" he said aloud in frustration. Despite what he'd told her, he had to admit that there were times when his job *was* exciting. That was partly the reason he loved it. Every day was different from the last, with new challenges to face, new problems to solve. Why would it have interested him otherwise? He didn't want a boring nine-to-five day job behind some desk, tapping computer keys until he went blind.

Nick had always wanted to be a policeman, even when he was a little kid. Now all of a sudden the time had come for him to question his decision. One reason he'd avoided it so long was because he knew, in the back of his mind, it was going to come down to a choice between the job he always wanted and the woman he'd always dreamed of.

But by the time he entered the freeway, Nick knew what he'd have to do. If giving up his job was the only way to keep Jessica safe, then he would simply have to give it up, period. If she kept insisting she wanted to be a part of his world, the only thing for him to do would be to change his world.

He sighed in resignation. Maybe it wouldn't be so bad. He'd put up with any job if it meant keeping Jessica safe and at his side. He'd just begun to relax when the sudden vibration of the pager at his belt startled him.

"Duty calls," he muttered, glancing at the familiar number. He automatically reached for the cellular phone he kept tucked under the front seat of his car and called the station.

"Nick Fox here," he said calmly, instinctively slipping from boyfriend mode into his professional police mode.

"Uh-huh," he said as Dub Harrison explained that the chief needed him for an important case that had just come up. "All right. I'm about ten minutes from the station now. I'll meet you there."

As Nick sped toward the station he suddenly remembered his vow to quit—for Jessica's sake. "Well," he reasoned, "it won't hurt to take one more job. I can keep Jessica out of harm's way that long."

Chapter Three

Beeeep!

As the horn blared, Elizabeth gasped and swerved away from yet another close call. The tears that kept filling her eyes were becoming a driving hazard.

This is crazy, she thought. *Maybe Nick was right. I shouldn't have driven back alone. I'm going to have an accident if I don't stop somewhere and get my emotions under control.*

With relief she noticed that the very next exit would take her to the beach. She flipped on her blinker and moved to the right-hand lane. A moment later she pulled from the freeway and onto the exit, making it to a parking lot without any further close calls.

All her life the Pacific Ocean had been her favorite retreat. The beach had been a place where she could go to recharge, a place where she could usually find calmness and serenity. Maybe today it would bring her peace.

As she stepped out of the Jeep she pulled loose the black comb from her French twist, letting her hair blow wildly in the wind. The salty sea air cooled her wet cheeks and filled her lungs. She longed to throw off her shoes and run down the beach, to feel the sunbaked sand on her bare feet and then splash through the cool wet surf. But she wasn't exactly dressed for it today. Instead she settled onto the top of the low rock wall that separated the parking area from the sand.

Maybe it was because the day had turned cool, or maybe it was because it was a Wednesday, but the beach wasn't crowded. She could see a man jogging with a dog in the distance; in the other direction a woman watched as two little children built a sand castle. Elizabeth had an entire section of beach practically to herself.

As she stared at the magnificence of the Pacific a calmness settled over her. There was something reassuring about the ocean. The endless vista of blue water meeting blue sky at the horizon. Earth and sea and air all making a big eternal circle that lasted forever in a way people couldn't.

"Good-bye, Gin Yung," she said aloud. "I'm sorry it had to end this way. I never meant to cause you any pain."

She swallowed the lump that rose in her throat. *I'm doing it again,* she thought. *Just like Nina said, I'm holding everything in. Denying what I feel.*

"Let it out," she could almost hear Nina saying. *"What's bothering you, girl? Let it out."*

"Good-bye, Todd," Elizabeth said, looking up into the sky.

Suddenly tears gushed from her eyes, and her body began to shake. *I've lost him forever,* she realized. *No more reliable, strong, wonderful Todd. What am I going to do without him?*

She shouldn't have been surprised at his words in the garden. In a way she'd known it would be inevitable. She'd known it ever since that night at the hospital, when they'd heard the news about Gin-Yung's tumor. The instant she'd seen the terror-stricken look in Todd's eyes, she'd known she'd lost him—again.

She wrapped her arms tightly around herself and closed her eyes against the pain. *I almost wish he'd never come back into my life at all,* she thought. But as Todd's sweet face appeared behind her closed eyelids, she knew that wasn't true.

"I take it all back," she whispered, opening her eyes and replacing Todd's image with the bright California sky. "I don't regret a single second of my time with Todd." If not for him, Elizabeth didn't know how she could have ever survived losing Tom.

Tom. She suddenly began to sob uncontrollably. *Why am I crying for Tom? He means nothing*

51

to me. I've been over him since Todd and I got back together! Haven't I? She covered her face with her hands, but it did little to hide the loud sniffling, sobbing noises she was making. *I don't care about Tom. I don't! He's stubborn and hot tempered and cruel. . . .*

Then why do I miss him so much?

"Oh, Tom! Why didn't you believe me?"

She cried until she couldn't cry any more.

Shhh, the ocean whispered as a wave rushed to shore. *Shhh.* Like a mother comforting a crying child, it sang a soothing lullaby.

Sitting there on the fence, with the wind drying the tears on her wet face, Elizabeth slowly regained control. She watched as wave after wave splashed against the beach in a foamy, white froth.

Every wave whispered for her to be calm. Then it slid back into the ocean, taking with it tiny bits of seaweed and shelled sea creatures, leaving the sandy beach smooth and clean.

Elizabeth closed her eyes and pretended the waves were washing over her own body, taking away all the debris of her shattered emotions, taking away the pain of losing Tom, Todd, and Gin-Yung. She tried to imagine her life as smooth as the golden sea-washed sand, ready for new footprints.

Todd was right about closure. She needed it. The time had come to reach out and close a few doors of her own.

Good-bye, Gin-Yung. Good-bye, Todd. Good-bye, Tom.

Closure. It sounded so final. Was it the end of the book? No, only Gin-Yung had reached the end. For Elizabeth it was only the beginning of a new chapter. Elizabeth would keep on living. She had a choice that Gin-Yung didn't have.

"My life is like the newly washed sand," she murmured. "I'm starting over." If fact, she'd already taken a step in that direction. Last week she had interviewed with the faculty sponsors of the campus newspaper, the *Sweet Valley Gazette,* and they'd accepted her. In today's sadness she'd almost forgotten that she would soon be starting a new job.

I'm going to be OK, she thought. *I still have so much to be thankful for. I have Jessica. I have my brother, Steven. I have wonderful parents. I have true friends like Nina. And I still have my journalism.*

With a final sniff and one last look at the ocean, Elizabeth headed back to the Jeep. Having no more Kleenex, she wiped her face on a sweatshirt that Jessica had left in the backseat. Her sister's messiness could come in handy sometimes.

With a lighter heart and a new attitude Elizabeth left the beach, merged into the traffic, and headed back to Sweet Valley University.

Back in her room in Dickenson Hall, Jessica

kicked off Elizabeth's black heels, sending one flying toward her overflowing closet and the other crash landing into a pile of dirty laundry. "Men!" she snarled. "I guess they all expect women to sit at home and knit socks or something. Well, not this woman!"

She stubbed her toe on her Western civ book and howled. "Stupid book!" She shoved it across the floor, hobbled over to her bed, and collapsed dramatically onto the jumble of clothing, shoes, cosmetics, and purple satin sheets.

I've had it, she thought when the pain in her toe subsided. *I'm tired of boring classes, this cramped, boring room, stupid, boring books, and this boring, boring,* boring *life! I want to have some excitement, some* fun!

Shoving a stack of fashion magazines out of the way, she grabbed the phone and quickly dialed Lila's number. Lila Fowler was her very best friend in the whole world; Jessica could always count on Lila to cheer her up. Maybe the two of them could go hang out at Theta house. After all, what was the sense in being a member of the most prestigious sorority on campus if you didn't take time to enjoy the fellowship and facilities it had to offer?

Yes, she decided. *That's exactly what I need.* Tea with her sorority sisters at Theta house could almost always bring Jessica out of a bad mood—although the mood she was in now would take a gallon of tea to wash away.

Come on, Lila, answer. I need you, she pleaded silently as the phone rang and rang in her ear. At the seventh ring Bruce finally answered. Jessica frowned. His was one of the last voices she wanted to hear. Just because Lila was totally infatuated with Mr. Supersnob didn't mean he had to hover over her day and night.

"Lila is resting, Jess," he said.

"I don't care. I want to talk to her. It's important."

"OK, I'll get her," he said as if he were doing Jessica an immense favor. "Just a minute."

Jessica was beginning to suspect that Bruce had run out for a quick game of tennis instead just before Lila's voice finally came over the line.

"What is it, Jess? I'm sort of tired," she said weakly.

"Me too. That's why I'm calling. I'm tired of sitting around this boring dorm. I thought we could do something this afternoon. Do you want to hang out at Theta house?"

"Hmmm . . . well, actually, Jess—"

Jessica coughed loudly into the phone. She hated being told no in the best of times, but right now she didn't think she could bear Lila's rejection. "Or," she amended quickly, "we could go to the Red Lion, have a cappuccino, and get caught up on the latest gossip."

"Ummm, I really can't. I'm just too strung out. That funeral this morning really took it out of me."

"I noticed you were pretty upset." *So upset, you didn't even speak to your best friend, namely me,* Jessica added mentally.

"Oh, Jessica, it was simply awful! I was sad about Gin-Yung and everything, but when I looked around at all the sad faces and heard all that dreary music and smelled those flowers, I started thinking about Tisiano. It was like I was going through his funeral all over again." She lowered her voice to a whisper. "Then I started feeling guilty because I was with Bruce and haven't even been thinking about Tisiano much lately."

Jessica searched through her mind for a way to change the subject. Tisiano di Mondicci had been a part of her best friend's life that she had been unable to share. While Lila was living it up in Europe as the countess di Mondicci, Jessica was at SVU, trying to cope with her own disastrous marriage and annulment. Although Jessica knew Lila had been wildly in love with Tisiano, the whole thing always seemed unreal to her.

Besides, Jessica didn't want to dwell on the past. She and Lila had both had more than their share of heartbreaks. Jessica was glad she had been around to help Lila get over Tisiano's death when she'd returned to Sweet Valley, but now wasn't the time to drag all that back up. She didn't want to think about sad things. She especially didn't want to think any more about death.

"Oh. Hey, you won't believe the dish I've

got!" Jessica blurted, changing the subject. "Liz and Todd broke up again." Groaning internally, she thought, *See how boring my life has become? It's pretty bad when the only juicy thing I can come up with is about* Elizabeth's *boring love life.*

"That's too bad," Lila said. "They were always so cute together, although I always thought Tom Watts was the better catch."

Jessica twisted the phone cord around her finger. What did it matter? Tom and Todd were about the same as far as she was concerned. Both were major hunks, but both ranked way up there on the dullness scale. Neither of them was half as interesting as Nick. *Maybe I should pick out Liz's next boyfriend for her,* she thought with a giggle.

"Jessica, I'm glad you called, but I'm going to have to let you go; I was—"

"Listen," Jessica interrupted. "If you don't feel like going out today, maybe we could do something tomorrow. I'm having breakfast with Nick, and then I have to go to my Western civ class, but after that I'm free. We could go to the mall." Shopping was one activity that never failed to lift Jessica's spirits.

"Well, it sounds like fun, but I'm afraid Bruce and I already have plans. We're going to the Verona Springs Country Club." Lila's voice seemed to brighten suddenly. "We decided to treat ourselves to a little R-and-R, you know what I mean?

We need to get away from campus and away from . . . other things."

"I totally know what you mean. I've been thinking the exact same thing. I wish I had someplace like the Verona Springs Country Club to escape to. I hear it's a totally chic place. Is it true they have two pools?"

"Yes, one indoor and one outdoor. Both are Olympic size."

"Fantastic. You know, my tan could *really* use some work. I haven't been to the beach in *ages*. And the pool on campus is always so grungy and crowded. I *hate* going there."

"I know what you mean. I haven't been there since the Sigmas and Thetas held that charity float-a-thon."

"Oh, don't mention that. My hair was green for a week from the chlorine."

"I remember. I thought we'd never get you back to normal. Izzy must've poured everything on your head from tomato juice to Winston's car soap."

Jessica tapped her foot impatiently. She didn't want to talk about hair. She wanted to get Lila back on the subject of the country club. If she was crafty, maybe she could get Lila to invite her along.

"I'll bet Bruce joined the country club so he'd have a fresh crop of suckers to play tennis with," Jessica said. "They do have tennis courts, don't they?"

"Six of them. They have *everything*: pools, tennis courts, a world-renowned golf course, a hot tub, a weight room with a trainer always on duty, a five-star restaurant, a private ballroom for parties. . . . I couldn't even begin to list all the amenities."

"Don't you get *bored* out there all by yourself while Bruce spends all his time on the tennis court?" Jessica asked, a sly smile spreading across her face.

"No, silly. If Bruce wants to play tennis, then I'll play with him. Anyway, I could never be bored at Verona Springs," Lila said. "It's really the most wonderful place, Jess. There are gardens to walk in, big comfy lounges where you can visit with friends or curl up with a magazine. I love it. I could just *live* there!"

Jessica scowled in annoyance. "I'm surprised you never mentioned it to me before, Li. I didn't even know you and Bruce were members."

"We haven't been long. Right now Bruce and I are members of the Couples-Only section, but we're working on upping our membership."

"What?"

"Well, there are members, and there are *members,* if you know what I mean."

"No, Lila. I don't have a clue."

Lila sighed in apparent exasperation. "The club is sort of divided up into different levels of membership. Of course, all the members are special, but then there's the Couples-Only section, with young couples like Bruce and me. And then the most exclusive group is the VIP Circle."

La-di-da, Jessica thought. "Well, what do they do? Get to wear funny hats or special badges or something?" Jessica asked, no longer attempting to hide her irritation. Lila had been a real snob in high school, but her attitude had improved a lot since she'd been in college. Suddenly it seemed as if she was reverting back to her old, snobby ways.

This is Bruce Patman's influence, Jessica realized. She'd had a bad feeling something like this would happen ever since the day Lila and Bruce got together. He was the snobbiest of snobs. Always had been, always would be. Jessica had even fallen for his playboy charms once back in high school—what a fiasco that had been!

"No badges, Jess. But there are certain sections of the club open only to the VIP Circle."

"Like what?"

"Like the whole third floor, for one."

"And what's on the third floor?"

"I don't know, Jess. I'm not in the VIP Circle—*yet*. But I fully intend to be."

Jessica's frustration level reached its peak. *What's the matter with everyone today? Can't anyone take a hint?* she thought. *Well, subtlety has never been my style anyway.* "Lila, I imagine that country club of yours allows *guests,* doesn't it?" she asked blatantly.

"Well, of *course* it does. If someone wants to put a friend up for membership, they usually bring them out as guests first and show them around. In fact, that's how it happened that Bruce and I joined. I ran into this girl I used to know, Pepper Danforth? She and I used to take riding lessons together back in junior high. Well, we got to talking, and she mentioned the club. Pepper was simply flabbergasted to think that Bruce and I weren't members."

Jessica rolled her eyes. "I thought you always hated places like that. Why would you want to hang around a bunch of blue-haired old ladies drinking tea and eating crumpets?"

"It's not like that, Jess. I guess there are a few older members around, but no one in the Couples-Only section is old. You'd love it."

"Yes, I probably *would*," Jessica said, tossing aside her very last drop of subtlety for the day. "So why don't you invite me along as your guest? Remember how we used to go to your father's country club back in—"

"This isn't my father's country club, Jessica. And I would invite you, really I would, but as I said, Bruce and I belong to the Couples-Only section. You simply couldn't go there without a date."

Jessica's jaw dropped. "Yoo-hoo! News bulletin time, Lila. In case you've been too busy to notice, I've *got* a boyfriend. Remember Nick?"

"Of course I remember Nick, but—"

"But what?" Jessica said, practically daring Lila to continue.

"Well . . . Nick is hardly the country club type, now, is he?"

For one of the few times in her life, Jessica was speechless. She couldn't believe her best friend was doing this to her. While she sat there, staring at the phone, Lila continued to chatter on and on in a sickeningly superior tone about her precious country club.

". . . and I looked closer, and it was a Lalique vase! And that's not all, Jessica. You should see the antiques and paintings in the lounges. I hear the VIP lounge has a Matisse *and* a Renoir. Isn't it simply divine?"

What happened to the Lila who was too tired to talk a moment ago? Jessica wondered.

". . . and they have a formal Elizabethan garden with every kind of flower you can imagine."

"Pardon me while I yawn."

Lila laughed. "Oh, c'mon. You're just jealous. Verona Springs is *so* exciting—"

"Speaking of exciting," Jessica interrupted, "the most wonderful thing has happened to me today. Nick has agreed to let me go on one of his stakeouts with him."

Jessica winced at her lie. *Well, it isn't really a lie,* she told herself. *Just more of a prediction. Nick will cave in eventually. I know he will.*

"That's nice, Jess," Lila said in a tone that let Jessica know she thought it was anything but.

When Lila returned to jabbering about the wonders of Verona Springs, Jessica cut her off. "Well, I'd better let you go. You probably have tons of preparing to do for your day at the *ca-lub*." Jessica sarcastically exaggerated the word into two weighty syllables, but Lila didn't seem to notice. She was probably preoccupied with planning the perfect outfit.

After Jessica dropped the receiver noisily back into its cradle, she began to imagine herself making a splash at the Verona Springs Country Club. She could just see herself dressed in a slinky designer gown, sitting on a moonlit terrace, overlooking the glittering Verona Springs Reservoir, eating caviar and drinking champagne. It'd be great to have all that money and luxury.

She looked around at the cramped, messy dorm room—well, her half was cramped and messy; Elizabeth's half was cramped and clean. Squeaky clean. So clean, it was practically sterile. But clean or messy, the crowded room was hardly more than a cell. And if she didn't get out of there soon, she'd go stir-crazy.

Jessica closed her eyes and dreamed up another club fantasy. In this version she saw herself stepping out of a limo and dashing across the lawn in tennis whites that showed off her perfect tan. Throngs of club members welcomed her with happy shouts. She would be the most popular person in the club. Everyone would love her.

Wouldn't it be a hoot if I was invited into that VIP Circle and Lila wasn't? she thought, imagining herself waltzing past Lila and Bruce with her nose in the air and stepping onto the private elevator that would take her to the unknown heights of snobdom. Wouldn't that freeze Lila's gorgeous face in a mask of fury? Jessica leaned back and smiled at the image.

But the moment she tried to drop Nick into the fantasy, the scene faded away. Lila was right— Nick *didn't* fit in. For a moment Jessica felt a pang of resentment, but it quickly dissolved. She didn't *want* Nick to be a rich snob. *That type bores me to tears,* she realized. *Nick is much more exciting than the Bruce Patman type.* She brushed aside the country club fantasies like cookie crumbs. *Lila, you can have Bruce Patman and your fancy club. I'll stick with Nick Fox and pure excitement, thank you very much.*

Jessica jumped in front of the mirror and began practicing her *Charlie's Angels*-inspired gun stance. *When Nick caves in and asks me to be his partner, will he give me a gun?* she wondered. *If he does, should I hold it with one hand or two?*

She spun toward the closet as if someone had just tried to get the jump on her. *Maybe I should hold it one-handed and sideways.* She copied the pose she'd seen in countless movies. *No, that's way too psycho for me.* She crouched slightly and held both hands out in front of her. *Yes, this is more like it. The two-handed grip is totally my style.* She took aim, shot, and dramatically blew imaginary smoke from the tips of her fingers.

"Thanks for coming in on your day off, Nick."

"No problem, Chief," Nick said. He pulled off his suit coat and draped it over the back of the chair. "What's going on? Dub said something about a floater."

Chief Wallace leaned against his battered desk and hooked his thumbs in his red suspenders.

"A body was found early last week, floating facedown in the reservoir right next to the golf course at the Verona Springs Country Club."

"Last week?" Nick asked incredulously. "And we're just now learning about it?"

"Well, the folks at the country club haven't exactly been eager for publicity. And besides, the first report that came in said it was an accidental drowning."

"But now . . . ?" Nick prodded, leaning forward in his chair.

"But now the medical examiner has ruled it a homicide. The crime scene unit has been over the entire area with a fine-tooth comb. We've got a report of their findings here." He leaned across the desk and grabbed a manila envelope. "These are the photos."

As Chief Wallace spread the stark pictures across his desk Nick unwrapped a stick of chewing gum, popped it into his mouth, and tucked the foil into his pocket. Looking at crime scene photos always left a bad taste in his mouth—literally.

Finished, the chief ran a hand through his thinning hair, waddled around behind his desk, and sat down. He leaned forward and tapped the first photo with a thick, stubby finger. "The body was identified as a club employee, a caddy. Let's see," he said, shuffling through the papers in a new file folder. "Here, his name was . . . Dwayne Mendoza. He was a student at Sweet Valley University. You ever hear of him?"

Nick shook his head.

"One of the club's groundskeepers found him," the chief continued. "He said he figured the caddies must have had a little party after hours in the clubhouse, and the kid drank too much, fell in the lake, and drowned. An uncle of the victim, also employed by the club, claimed the kid didn't drink. But the first officer on the scene was thinking, What do relatives know about teenagers, right? That's why he called it in as an accidental drowning. Anyway, the toxicology reports confirmed the old man's story—there wasn't a drop of alcohol in the kid's blood."

"So what about suspects?"

"Officially there's one. As soon as the medical examiner pointed out that the injuries Mendoza

66

had suffered were inconsistent with a fall into the lake—"

"What injuries?" Nick interrupted.

Again Chief Wallace consulted the file. "Uh . . . contusions, various bruises on face and torso, and a fractured jaw."

"So Mendoza was beaten before he went into the water?"

"Badly, I'd say."

"Who's the suspect?"

"Well, as I was saying. When the ME ruled out accidental death, witnesses started coming out of the woodwork. Several club members suddenly remembered seeing Mendoza fighting with another caddy the day before."

Again the chief fumbled with the stack of loose papers. "Brandon Phillips, also an SVU student."

Nick shrugged to indicate that he'd never run across that name in his dealings on campus either. "Just because they had an argument doesn't necessarily mean Phillips smacked Mendoza in the jaw and drowned him."

"That's exactly what Phillips said. He admitted arguing with Mendoza. Said they'd even exchanged a few punches. But according to him, the last time he saw Mendoza, he was alive and well."

"That's all they've got to go on?"

"Well, the fight gives him motive, not to mention the fact that Mendoza's watch and wallet were found in Phillips's locker."

"Was there any cash in the wallet?"

"About forty bucks."

"And they're certain it was Mendoza's watch?"

"Phillips admits it himself. But he swears he's being set up. Phillips's fingerprints weren't found on either piece of evidence. They're both clean."

Nick shrugged. "Sounds like a weak case both for and against the guy. Still, why would a caddy want to rob another caddy when there are rich kids left and right at that place?"

"Wait—there's one more link to Phillips. An eyewitness claims he saw Phillips leaving the club late the night of the murder, at a time when he would've had no reason to be there."

Nick shook his head. "That's still pretty circumstantial."

"Exactly. The kid claims he got a call to come to the club and pick up a check he was owed. And while the excuse is pretty shaky, that's all we've got to go on, I'm afraid."

Nick examined the photos again. "Was Phillips arrested?"

"He's being held on suspicion, but unless something turns up soon, he'll be charged with murder one."

"What did the questioning officer think about Phillips?"

"Hmmm," the chief began, scratching his chin. "It's here somewhere, but I know Bob Henderson over at homicide doesn't think the kid had anything to do with it. He thinks there's something rotten going on at the club. He told his men to dig around, but no matter where they looked, the Verona Springs Country Club members kept coming out with their noses squeaky clean. Bob suspects at the very least that someone over there is covering up information."

"It sounds suspicious, sir, but why call on us? What do they want with a vice detective?"

"What it boils down to is, there are too many rich, influential members with too much political pull for homicide to start stepping on toes before they know exactly what's going on. And they've decided the only way to find out what's going on is to put someone undercover at the club."

"What about Chris Devonshire? With his family connections, he'd be perfect to go undercover with those snooty country club types. You know me. I work with the kids at the college, the drug scene, the illegal IDs, the car thieves. I'm not exactly the country club type."

"But you can be. I know you, Fox. I figure you'll blend in with the angels on judgment day if it's to your advantage. You're the best undercover man I've got. Besides, it'd be too risky to send Chris. Too many people might know him."

"I'll need a cover and a way in. Don't you have to be invited to be a member of a club like this?"

"I'm working on a connection right now. I'm pretty sure Judge Pettigrew will give us a way in.

I'll have to let you know the details later."

As he started out the door Nick paused, re-membering his vow to quit police work for Jessica's sake. *Should I tell the chief that this is my last case?* he wondered. *No. If I do, he might lose confidence in me. He might think I'll be too lax and not give the job the concentration it deserves. I'd better wait until after this case is settled.*

Chapter Four

I can't believe I'm actually doing this! Elizabeth thought as she whipped her Jeep into the staff-only parking space in front of the communications building Thursday morning. *I'm actually leaving WSVU—for good.* She tugged up the sleeve of her baggy SVU sweatshirt and glanced at her watch to make sure she was on schedule. It was important that she get inside the campus television station and clear out her things before Tom showed up. *I still have plenty of time,* she assured herself. Being as familiar with his class schedule as she was with her own, she knew that he'd be in logic class for the next hour.

Scott Sinclair waved heartily and jogged up beside the Jeep before she got her door opened. His chin-length, sun-streaked hair and healthy, tanned complexion were a bit misleading. By appearance he seemed to be the outdoorsy, hang-out-at-the-beach

71

type, but since Elizabeth had gotten to know him, she knew he was not only an intellectual but also a really serious journalism major.

"Here I am," he announced, "nine-oh-five on the dot, as promised." His crystalline blue eyes gleamed with pleasure. He opened the door for her and took her hand as she stepped down.

"It's sweet of you to help me move my things, Scott."

"What else could I do? After all, I feel responsible. I'm the one who talked you into leaving the glitter and glitz of the TV world for the real world of newspaper journalism."

Elizabeth shook her head. "Not true. Although you may have been with me when I made the decision to quit WSVU and go to work at the paper, you were only the little spark that got me moving. I'd been thinking about a change for a long time. I just never had the courage to do anything about it until you came along."

"OK, then." Scott walked backward in a jerky circle as if he were caught on a rewinding videotape. "I feel responsible," he began again. "After all, I'm the one who sparked you into finally carrying out your plans to leave the glitter and—"

"OK, OK, I get the picture. Now that I've got you suffering from guilt, let's see if those muscles of yours are good for anything but looks."

Scott and Elizabeth crossed the quiet lobby of the station and went down the hall to the private office Elizabeth had once shared with Tom.

Elizabeth paused in the doorway. A lump came into her throat as she looked at the cozy little room where she and Tom had spent so many late nights working . . . and sometimes not working.

"What's wrong?" Scott asked. "No second thoughts, I hope."

"No. I'm just thinking I'm glad Tom's not here."

"He doesn't know you're leaving, does he?"

"No, I don't think so; not that I owe him an explanation or anything. I cleared it with Professor Sedder. As head of the communications department *he's* actually the person in charge of the station, not Tom."

"Yeah, right. Tell Tom that. You should have heard him squawking when I quit. Was Sedder cool about it?"

"He said he understood but that they'd miss me around here."

"Well, WSVU's loss is the *Gazette's* gain." Scott edged past Elizabeth into the room. "I'll probably be the hero of the paper when they find out what a great writer you are."

"You're too flattering."

"It's not flattery. I'm serious. Haven't I told you from the start that you're way too talented to waste your time on TV reporting?"

Elizabeth blushed. "Yes, and you've almost got me convinced." She laughed lightly to cover her

73

embarrassment, but Scott didn't seem to realize she was joking.

"Good. That's what I've been trying to do." He gazed at her until she was forced to look away.

"Well, why don't we get started?" She pointed to a low, beat-up file cabinet. "Everything in that file drawer is mine. If you'll box up those files, I'll empty these drawers and sort through that cabinet by Tom's desk."

"Listen, Elizabeth, about Tom. What's up with you two? I know you told me that you had a falling-out, but if we're going to work together, maybe you'd better fill me in."

Elizabeth stiffened. This sudden conversational turn was worse than his embarrassing flattery. "Nothing is going on."

"Something is. The other day when I stopped by the station to give you those notes from Sedder's lecture—you know, the one about ethics in journalism—Tom was the only one here. When I asked if he'd seen you, I thought the guy would bite my head off. Mentioning your name around him is like slapping a bull on the nose with a smelly red gym towel."

Elizabeth looked at Scott, then away. She knew exactly what he meant. These days when people mentioned Tom, it affected her the same way. She slowly flipped through a stack of papers, decided they weren't worth keeping, and tossed them into the wastebasket. "Tom's got some problems right now that he needs to work out."

"Well, he shouldn't take them out on you. Or me, for that matter."

"No, he shouldn't," Elizabeth agreed in a strained voice.

"So what's his problem?"

Elizabeth threw up her hands in exasperation. "Are all the *Gazette*'s reporters this nosy?"

"Only the best ones."

Elizabeth dropped her arms and exhaled slowly. "Listen, Scott, it's not something I want to talk about. But like you said, if we're going to be working together, I guess you might as well know. Tom and I have a lot of hard feelings between us right now. We were a couple—a perfectly matched couple, or so I thought. But then something happened, and we broke up."

"What happened?"

Elizabeth didn't know why she kept on talking. She could have left it at that, but Scott was so easy to talk to. He seemed to listen to her with his whole body. She found it flattering that anyone would be that interested in her life, a life that, in Jessica's immortal words, was "boring, boring, boring."

"It doesn't matter what happened—not really," she said. "But it boiled down to the fact that Tom didn't trust me or have enough confidence in our relationship. He jumped to a lot of conclusions and showed a side of himself that I never knew he had. Now not only are we no longer dating, but we're no longer *speaking*. And it's a little hard to work in the field of communications with someone you can't communicate with."

Scott scooted closer, his blue eyes concerned. "Maybe you two should talk it out."

"Believe me, I tried. For weeks I called him, left notes, and even chased him all over campus, trying to get him to talk to me. But every time I'd try to talk, he'd only attack me. He called me names and accused me of everything from jealousy to cheating to backstabbing. He embarrassed me so many times, I can't count them all." Elizabeth sucked in a deep breath, surprised at her confessional state. "This move to the *Gazette* is good for me in more ways than one."

"Yeah, it sounds like you need to make a clean break with the past."

"Something like that."

Was it her imagination, or did Scott look happier than ever? Confused, Elizabeth pulled a fat folder from the bottom drawer. It held the records she'd kept while she and Tom had been working on the athletics recruiting scandal. *Maybe Tom hates me now,* she told herself, *but no one can deny the fact that we did some powerful reporting together.*

In a way she hated to leave the station. So many of her good college memories involved this very room. She looked fondly at the sagging, lumpy couch where she and Tom had taken so many work breaks. When she considered how much kissing they'd done on that couch, it was a wonder they'd ever gotten a story finished. But they had. And they both had the awards and clippings to prove it.

As bittersweet memories threatened to overpower her she threw the last of her papers into a cardboard box and slammed the desk drawer shut.

"That's that," she said, picking up her desk blotter and slipping it under her arm.

Scott gave the file drawer a kick shut. "I'm done too."

"Let's get outta here." She hurried through the office door as Scott held it open. Her throat was way too tight to even say thank you.

Just before they reached the exit doors, Elizabeth stopped so suddenly, Scott nearly tripped over her. "Oh, wait," she blurted, letting the box she was holding slide to the floor. "I forgot something." She set the desk blotter on top of the pile. "My favorite mug. You wait here. I'll be right back."

She ran back down the deserted hallway and grabbed her News Hound mug from the coffee cart. Then she stopped and looked around one last time. It was best that Scott wasn't there while she said her private, final good-bye.

"Good-bye, WSVU," she murmured weakly, walking over to her ex-boyfriend's desk. "We were

77

a great team, Tom." She ran her hands over the orderly but heaping stack of tapes and papers that lay there. She could tell Tom was going to be very busy at the station without her. *Who is going to take my place?* she wondered.

The image of Dana Upshaw suddenly popped into her mind. She shook her head rapidly. *At the station, I mean. I guess I've already been replaced in the other vacancy I left in his life.* As tears threatened to fall she swallowed them back.

"It wasn't my fault. I didn't throw away our love, Tom. You did," she said to his vacant desk chair.

She took one last lingering look around before turning off the light and shutting the door on another chapter of her life.

As much as it annoyed Tom to have someone not show up for an appointment—especially one he'd had to get up early for—Tom had convinced himself that his logic professor's absence from class was a stroke of good luck. He was up and out and determined to use his newfound time wisely. There was so much work that needed to be done at the station, it was unbelievable. He hadn't exactly been doing a bang-up job as station manager of WSVU lately. In fact, the station seemed to be falling apart. Between his neglect and Elizabeth's total absence, nothing was getting done. And that was before the two new interns quit!

He paused outside the station and squinted at the sunlight reflecting off the building's glass front. Were his eyes deceiving him, or was that really Elizabeth standing beside her Jeep? His heart began racing even before he hastened his steps. It really *was* her! Her jeans and soft sweatshirt, her bouncing blond ponytail . . . she looked just the way he'd imagined her whenever he'd pictured their reunion. *She's come to talk to me about my apology letter— at last!*

Then suddenly he realized she wasn't alone. Some guy was holding the door for her—that intern who'd quit after only a week!

Tom darted behind a row of bushes so they couldn't see him. *What was his name? Steve? Shawn? No, Scott . . . Scott something or other. And he's climbing into her red Jeep as if he has every right to be there!*

His face flushed red with anger. *Where's her precious Wilkins? I thought the two of them were joined at the hip these days, but nope, here she is with some other guy. I guess things aren't so great in paradise—or maybe she's simply expanding her options.*

Although he felt foolish crouching in the bushes, Tom waited until the Jeep was out of sight before going into the WSVU building. He slammed the door of the outer office so hard, the tapes lining the wall shelves rattled together noisily. Stepping into the office he and Elizabeth had shared, he was fully prepared to vent his fury on the first available article small enough for him to throw or low enough for him to kick. But seeing Elizabeth's vacant desk caught him by surprise. The air escaped his lungs and took the anger with it, leaving only sadness.

Although tidy, Elizabeth's desk had always shown signs of her presence. But now everything was gone: the handmade vase with the fake sunflower, the photo cube with the pictures of her sister, Jessica, her brother, Steven, her mom and dad, and even a shot of her golden retriever, Prince Albert, with a Santa cap on his head.

He sank into her desk chair and laid his head on his arms on her bare desk. Gone. All gone. No funny reminders tacked to the memo board. No sunflower-patterned blotter, no flowered mug full of sharpened pencils. Even the Con-Tact paper that she'd put on the side of the file cabinet had been peeled away. It lay crumpled in the trash can.

She had left without even saying good-bye. And she still hadn't answered his letter. *But maybe she has,* Tom thought hopefully. *Maybe she left me a note!*

One by one he jerked open each desk drawer—feeling deep into the backs of the drawers in case the note had fallen beyond reach. He ran his hand along the empty shelf above the desk, but he found nothing, not even dust.

On nearly numb legs Tom stumbled over to his own desk and dropped into his chair. He looked at the pile of work waiting for him and shook his head. He didn't feel like facing it now. He ran his hands through his hair and pressed his scalp with his fingertips. He felt as if his head was about to explode.

It's just not like Elizabeth to blatantly ignore an apology, he told himself. *Not like her at all.* He could see that she might not be able to forgive him—after all, he'd said and done some pretty awful things, but the least she could've said was, "Tom, I got your note. I hate you." Even *that* would have been better than her pretending he didn't exist. *Something must be wrong. Elizabeth is too kindhearted to keep anyone dangling like this— even someone she hates.*

He walked over to the rickety wheeled cart where the coffeepot stood. No one had thought to make a pot in ages. The stained carafe just lay there, empty, beside a couple of coffee mugs. Elizabeth's News Hound mug, the one with the comical puppy face that he'd bought for her at the broadcasters' convention in Las Vegas, was gone.

He cupped his hands around his mouth. "Elizabeth Wakefield has left the building," he declared in a corny announcer voice, but his tone was bitter and humorless.

He slammed his fist into the palm of his other hand.

Why, Elizabeth? he pleaded silently. *Why are you doing this to me?* Tom felt the anger rising back up his throat. "I've gotta get out of here," he muttered.

As he headed out the glass doors of WSVU and toward his dorm, each step became faster and faster until he was jogging, then running. Still he couldn't escape his thoughts. Even the slap of his tennis shoes on the concrete seemed to say, *"Gone, gone, gone . . ."* Each jarring step seemed to knock a little of the sadness from him and replace it with anger.

He stomped up to his dorm room and threw open the door. His anger was now bubbling over. *Apparently it wasn't hard for her to forget me overnight,* he realized. *She just wiped me out of her brain like an Etch-A-Sketch picture. Maybe she's forgotten Wilkins too. Maybe she has a whole string of new guys by now. Well, I can get along without her just as easily as she can get along without me. I'll show Elizabeth Wakefield that she can't ruin my life.*

Plopping into his desk chair, he stared at the phone. "If she doesn't care, then neither do I." He snatched up the receiver and began stabbing at the numbers. As the rings buzzed in his ear he rummaged in the wastebasket beside his desk.

"Dana? Hi! It's me, Tom . . . listen. I'm calling to apologize for how I acted the other day. It was inexcusable, I know, but I was ticked off about some stuff at the station and . . ."

He paused to give Dana Upshaw time to scold him for breaking their last date. He knew that he deserved whatever insults she wanted throw at him. *Ah, here's what I'm looking for,* he said silently. Holding the receiver between his chin and shoulder, he plucked Mr. Conroy's letter from the wastebasket, extracted the two membership applications from the envelope, and tossed the rest back into the trash where it belonged.

"Listen, Dana," he began. "I think I know how I can make it up to you. Have you ever heard of the Verona Springs Country Club? . . . You have? I thought so. Well, I just happen to have a membership right here with your name on it."

"That'll be great, sweetheart," Dana Upshaw cooed. "I can hardly wait till Sunday." As excited as she was, she hoped she'd managed to balance just the right amount of scolding with plenty of flattery and flirting. She didn't want to be a total pushover, but a guy like Tom Watts took careful handling. "OK, bye-bye now," she purred. "I'm glad you called."

"Very, very glad," she shouted aloud after hanging up the phone. She dived onto the ratty old velvet couch, kicking her bare feet excitedly in the air.

Felicity Jonas, one of her roommates, watched calmly from the doorway. "Was that who I think it was?" she asked.

"Yes," she declared. She tossed back her long mahogany curls and smiled triumphantly.

"I told you he'd come crawling back."

"Well, I don't know if he's *crawling*, but I think we can safely say he's coming around, at the very least."

"It's about time the boy showed some sense. What did he say?"

"He's invited me to the Verona Springs Country Club."

"Whoa, you're kidding! I heard that place is harder to get into than a size-three girdle."

"Oh, Felicity, don't be so naive. All it takes is money."

"And connections."

"Well, whatever it takes, Tom evidently has it all because I'm not just going as a guest." Dana noted the rise of Felicity's left eyebrow. "He's giving me a *membership!*"

Felicity's gray eyes widened. "No way!"

"Yes way."

"Dana, maybe you shouldn't let yourself get all worked up about this. How do you know he's not going to break this date at the last minute just like he did last weekend? It seems I remember a *certain* cello player moping around this house for a week."

"He totally apologized for last weekend."

"Oh." Felicity rolled her eyes. "All righty, then, I guess that makes him Mr. Reliable." Felicity threw up her hands and went back into the kitchen.

Dana wrinkled her nose and stuck out her tongue at Felicity's retreating back. *OK, so maybe Tom hasn't been Mr. Reliable in the past, but he will be from now on. I have the insurance right here.* She snapped open her cello case and slipped her hand beneath the soft, plush lining. Carefully she pulled out Tom's apology letter to Elizabeth and unfolded it. Just the feel of the paper in her hand made her want to gag. It was the most pitiful example of groveling she'd ever seen. "'I'm so sorry, Elizabeth,'" she read dramatically, throwing the back of her hand against her forehead. "'I really would do anything for you. . . .'"

She walked to her bedroom and slammed the door. "'My life has been meaningless without you. . . . I've never stopped loving you. . . .'" She continued to recite her least favorite lines as she walked around the serape-covered water bed. "'I'm begging you, Elizabeth, please . . .'" Dana stopped in front of the mirror and mimed poking her finger down her throat. "Isn't that the most pathetic thing you've ever heard?" she asked her reflection. Then she folded the letter and tucked it safely into her jewelry box.

She had been absolutely right in intercepting this little love note. The moment she'd seen the envelope with Tom's handwriting lying on Elizabeth Wakefield's desk, she'd known it was trouble. Tom clearly didn't know what was good for him. If he couldn't see that his sick obsession for Elizabeth Wakefield was ruining his chance for happiness with her, then it was up to her to do something about it. A stupid blunder like this letter could very easily have reunited him with Little Miss Butter-wouldn't-melt-in-her-mouth, who was obviously gullible enough to fall for Tom's bucket of sap.

"And it's me he really loves," she said to her reflection. "I know it. He made it perfectly clear that afternoon at the beach." She closed her eyes and recalled the sensation of being in Tom's arms as the waves splashed at their feet. She could almost feel the ocean breeze on her face as she remembered how she'd broken away and run along the sandy shore. She could practically hear his laughter as he chased her.

Dana's breathing slowed, and a peaceful smile spread across her face. *I knew he would come back to me if I kept him out of Wakefield's clutches.* And the fact that he'd called her and asked her out again was proof that her plan was working. Tom was weakening. *Soon Elizabeth will be no more than a vague, bad memory to him, and Tom will be mine— all mine.*

Jessica jumped from the Jeep and dashed across the busy street to where Nick waited on the sidewalk. "Sorry I'm late," she said breathlessly. "I know you said you only have an hour."

"Forty-five minutes," he corrected her, looking

at his watch. "But it's my fault. I should've just met you at that little coffee shop on campus. I thought we'd have more time together if you met me here."

"That's OK." She wrapped his arm around her waist and leaned against him. "I'd rather be here than at the Red Lion any day." She turned up her nose at the thought of the crowded campus coffee shop, full of student clones wearing the same SVU T-shirts, carrying the same boring books, and airing their typical daily gripes about their professors. Being with Nick was much better, especially when they went places where his cop friends hung out.

The Mug Shot was one of those places. It was hardly more than a narrow, dingy diner with mediocre food, but it was only a half block from the police station, making it one of their frequent hangouts.

As she and Nick settled into a tattered booth against the back wall, Jessica thought of Lila lounging away at her country club. *Imagine what she'd think if she saw this place,* she thought with a grin. The wobbly tables didn't match the chairs. The stools at the counter leaned at precarious angles. And even in the dim lighting it was easy to see that the floor tiles were chipped and made up of at least seven different colors that most people would never consider combining. It was cramped and smelled like the inside of an old coffeepot.

I totally love it, Jessica thought. *I can almost feel*

the excitement in the air. She looked at the other customers. Some wore uniforms, some didn't. She wondered how many of them were actually police officers.

The Mug Shot's only attempt at decoration was its artwork, if it could be called that. From ceiling to floor the walls were plastered with large, yellowing posters sporting black-and-white photos of the diner's most frequent patrons. Each poster consisted of two photographs, a full-face photo and a profile photo with numbers beneath each, just like the mug shots taken at police stations. Below the pictures were huge letters reading *Wanted,* and below that were the fictitious names, crimes, and characteristics of the pictured felon.

A waitress appeared beside the table and flipped open her green pad. She looked at Jessica and lifted her artificially arched eyebrows as if that were some sort of international sign language for "What do you want?"

"We didn't get a menu," Jessica said.

The waitress cracked her gum and pointed to a chalkboard on the counter.

Nick grinned. "I guess I should have warned you. Until the menu changes at noon, you have your basic three breakfast choices."

"What do they have at noon?"

"Your basic three lunch specials."

"Oh." Jessica squinted at the scribbled writing.

"Trust me," the waitress said. "The pancakes are your safest bet."

"OK. I'll have the pancakes."

"Drink?"

"Coffee," Jessica said.

"I'll have the same. Coffee, pancakes, but add bacon—a double order."

Jessica scanned the wall over their table, reading the wanted posters. "Oh, look, Nick. It's Dub!"

She pointed to a poster that showed the familiar chubby face of Dub Harrison, one of the detectives who worked with Nick. "Wanted," Jessica read. "Rub-a-dub Dub." She stretched her neck to read Dub's alleged crimes. The front view showed his heavy five o'clock shadow, and the profile shot accentuated his double chin. She laughed. "He really looks like a crook in those pictures."

The waitress returned and poured coffee into two large, mismatched mugs.

"Has Dub ever seen that poster?" Jessica asked, grinning. She grabbed a packet of sweetener and shook it back and forth a few times before tearing the corner.

"Of course he has. Everybody posed for those shots, Jess. Harve, the owner, used to be a crime scene photographer."

"Used to be? You mean he quit? Why?" Jessica couldn't believe anyone would give up such an exciting job.

"I guess he found out there was more money in bad coffee and lumpy pancakes."

"Are you on a poster—" Jessica began, only to be interrupted by someone clearing his throat noisily. She looked up to see a tall, thin man holding two heaping plates of pancakes.

"I'll have you know, my pancakes aren't lumpy." The man set the plates on the table before them. He fixed a squinty stare in Nick's direction.

Nick blushed. "Harve, this is Jessica. Jess, this is Harvey Venchure, the owner of this fine establishment."

"And chef," Harvey added importantly. He wiped his hands on his apron before shaking Jessica's hand. "Enjoy," he said. "Oh, and Miss Jessica, you might find the poster over the booth behind you to be quite interesting." He gave Nick a smile that let him know he'd been paid back for the lumpy pancake comment.

Jessica scurried to her knees and looked over the back of the booth. "Nick! It's you!" She flopped back down in her seat. "I would never have recognized you with that long gray hair, beard, and those wire-rimmed glasses. You look like an old hippie."

"Oh, hush and eat your pancakes," Nick said, reaching for a carafe of syrup.

"Why does Dub look like Dub, and you don't look like you?" Jessica asked, helping herself to a piece of bacon from Nick's plate.

"None of us who frequently work undercover thought it'd be a good idea to have our pictures plastered on the wall of a cop bar."

"Oh yeah. So, do a lot of criminal types come in here?" Jessica peered around the room in search of suspicious faces.

Nick laughed. "No, probably not. But we didn't want to take any chances." He smacked her hand as she snatched another piece of bacon. "Stop that. If you wanted bacon, why didn't you order it?"

Jessica successfully grabbed the second piece and bit into it with a crunch. "If you didn't want to share, why'd you get a double order?"

"Because I'm starving, that's why. I was up half the night, working."

"Poor baby," she cooed. "I worked last night too. I went to the library."

Nick practically choked on his coffee. "Sorry," he said, wiping his lips. "It was too hot."

Jessica smirked. "You don't believe I went to the library, do you?"

"Uh, of *course* I do, sweetie. What happened? Did you get lost, or did you decide to be adventurous and explore unseen campus territory?"

"Don't tease. I've been to the library before. Elizabeth isn't the only Wakefield who's allowed inside. And if you must know, I was there because I was checking out a very important book."

When he didn't say anything for a few moments,

she set down her fork and stared into his teasing jade green eyes. "Well . . . aren't you going to ask me what book I got?"

He set down his own fork and grinned. "You're going to tell me anyway, aren't you?"

Jessica smiled and tossed her hair over her shoulder. "I got a very interesting book called *Being a Cop in Today's World*."

When Jessica saw that glazed look of bored irritation come over Nick's face, she quickly changed the subject.

"Oh, look, Nick, there's Barry." Jessica waved at one of the cops she'd met during one of her frequent visits to the Sweet Valley Police Station. "Is that his wife? I'll bet she's a great help to him."

"Who? Oh, you mean Kathy? Yeah, I guess so."

"I'll bet she goes everywhere with him, even when he's on a stakeout."

"No way, Jess. She's a—"

"Were you about to say *woman?*" Jessica snapped, narrowing her eyes. "I certainly hope not. Because if you think women can't be cops, you'd better open *your* eyes. Look at some of these photos. Look at the other customers. There are a lot of women in here, and they're *cops*. I would never have pegged you for a chauvinist, Nick Fox, but—"

"Jessica, calm down." Nick scooted farther

against the wall and seemed to be sinking into his seat, but Jessica didn't plan to let him charm her with his little-boy embarrassment.

She scooted her plate aside and leaned forward with her arms on the tabletop. "I guess if it was up to you, all women would be banned from police work. I can't believe you were actually going to say she couldn't go on a stakeout because she's a woman."

"I wasn't going to say *woman*, Jess. I was about to say *librarian*."

"Oh." Jessica deflated slightly and sank back into her seat. But she didn't let the embarrassment of her faux pas last long. "Well, anyway. I'm still right. There are a lot of female police officers in here."

Nick shook his head. "Jess, I know where this is going, so let's cut to the chase. Yes, there are lots of police officers who happen to be women, and that's fine. I respect them. That doesn't mean you can just wake up one morning and say, 'Today I think I'll be a cop.' The women on the force are trained police officers. They have spent countless hours in classes that teach them everything from how to handle guns to how to handle a hysterical old lady reporting a lost poodle."

"Well, I could get training too. I'm in college, aren't I? I could take classes in law enforcement just as easily as I take dumb old stuff like history and science."

"Your pancakes are getting cold." Nick slid Jessica's plate closer to her.

"Don't change the subject. I'm serious. I really think police work would be the perfect career for me."

"Why, Jess? Why on earth have you suddenly decided that? I thought you wanted to be a model. What happened to that idea?"

"I don't know." Jessica poked at her pancakes with her fork. "I just don't think it would be as exciting as being a cop."

"You know nothing about police work, Jess."

"I know. That's why I want you to take me around with you."

Nick rested his elbow on the table and dropped his forehead into the palm of his hand.

Undaunted, Jessica hurried on. "And don't try to give me that same old speech about police work not being exciting. That night at the chop shop, remember? What a rush! That was the most exciting, fun night I've ever had in my whole life."

"Fun? Jessica, that wasn't *fun*. That was a *disaster*. We were almost killed."

"Well, we weren't. We weren't even scratched. Besides, it wasn't *my* fault that creep came out of the office with that semiautomatic. Aren't you forgetting I saved your life?"

Nick looked at his watch. "Want more pancakes?"

"I'm *serious*, Nick." She reached across the table and jiggled his arm. "Choosing a career is an important step in somebody's life. Everybody I know was practically born knowing exactly what they wanted to be, but I wasn't. I've really had to think about this—a *lot*. Now, when I finally decide something, you should be happy for me. Or at least you could support me. All I'm asking is for you to take me along on one little bitty case. Just so I can be sure it's what I really want to do. When you think about it, it'd be for your own good."

"Oh, really? Please explain the warped logic that brought you to that conclusion."

"Think how awful it'd be if I quit college, went to all the trouble of going to the police academy, and then found out I didn't want to be a police officer at all. My whole future would be ruined, and my parents would probably blame *you*."

Nick gulped. "Me?"

"They know how susceptible I am to gorgeous, sexy, green-eyed guys."

Visibly relaxing, Nick laughed. "You're crazy, you know that?" He leaned across the table and kissed her.

Yes! Jessica thought excitedly. *Victory is mine!* "Does that mean you'll let me come with you?"

"That was a kiss, sweetheart. It means I love you."

She flashed him a grin that brought out her dimple. "I know you love me, but can I be your partner? Please? You won't regret it, I promise."

"I'll think about it, Jess," he said weakly. "Give me a little time to consider what I'm getting myself into."

Jessica began to bounce up and down with glee, shaking their booth and the one next to them—vacant, luckily. *He's caving in, I know he is. He loves me way too much to ever say no. We're going to be the greatest crime-fighting team since Batman and Robin!*

Chapter Five

"I let you win," Lila confessed with a laugh as Bruce bounded over the net, swinging his tennis racket like a madman.

"Dream on," he said, sweeping her up into a sweaty hug. "You were beaten fairly and squarely, and quite decisively, I might add. All those years with my tennis coach, Pablo, have finally paid off."

"For Pablo, maybe. I heard he's driving a Jag now—paid for by your extra lessons alone, I believe."

"Not true. He drives a simple, ordinary Lexus."

Lila giggled at Bruce's mock indignation. She loved the way he looked in tennis whites. They showed off his lean, tanned muscles to perfection.

He kissed her on the tip of the nose. "But come on, admit it. I did win, didn't I?"

"Yes, you won. . . ." Lila pried herself away

from Bruce's embrace and wiped her nose with the sweatband on her left wrist. "But I still let you," she added after he'd jogged a safe distance away.

That's another way we're so alike, Lila thought. Neither of them liked to lose, but this one time Lila didn't care. She hadn't exactly let him win, but she hadn't played her hardest either. Getting sweaty and tired didn't fit in with her plans for the rest of the day. She wanted to look her best when they "accidentally" bumped into Pepper Danforth. Lila was certain that if she could broach the subject carefully, Pepper would support her and Bruce in becoming members of the VIP Circle.

"It's great being able to play here on the Couples-Only court, isn't it?" Bruce peeled off his headband and tossed it, along with a matching towel, into a monogrammed bag. "There's never a crowd. Not like at school where you have to wait for a court. I love it."

"Well, as the old saying goes, 'Rank has its privileges.'"

"I thought it was, 'Money has its privileges.'"

Lila shrugged. "Same difference."

Bruce shouldered his racket, opened the gate, and motioned for Lila to precede him out to the brick-lined pathway that led back to the clubhouse. "Beauty before athletic prowess."

"Ha. You are *so* witty today, darling."

Bruce frowned at her. "And you are certainly in a strange mood."

"Am I? I'm sorry. It's just that I'm nervous about running into Pepper."

Bruce rolled his blue eyes. "Why?"

"You know how important this membership is to me."

"Li, we're already members of the club. They can't toss us out because Pepper Danforth disapproves of your earrings or something."

"What's wrong with my earrings?" Lila asked. Her free hand flew instinctively to the gold-and-sapphire hoop at her earlobe. "They're too gaudy, aren't they? Do you think I should have gone with the diamond studs?" Her mouth hardened into a line. "Oh yes, I should have. I should have worn my simple one-carat diamond studs."

"Don't be silly. Your earrings are fine. I was just using that as an example."

His apparent amusement irritated her. "Well, don't," she snapped. "I'm serious about this membership thing."

"As I said before, we're already members."

"But we aren't part of the VIP Circle." Lila swung her racket at a nearby bush, sending a shower of azalea petals onto the path. "Doesn't it bother you that we're excluded from a part of the club?"

"Now that you put it that way, I guess it does, but—"

"Well, it bothers me. I can't stand it." She pouted. Maybe Bruce didn't understand her as well as she'd thought. But she didn't feel like explaining, not right now. *All my life my family has forced me to attend public school and regular-kid camps,* she thought. *It's humiliating. It's like they were trying to turn me into somebody else. I'm tired of denying who I really am. I belong here.* "I have to get us into the VIP Circle, Bruce. I just have to," she finished simply.

"OK, sweetheart. I'm sure if you want in, we'll get in. After all, why shouldn't we? We're both rich and gorgeous." He smirked sarcastically.

"Look. If you aren't going to be serious about this, then just don't talk to me!" Lila hurried several steps ahead of him.

"I *am* serious. Really. We both have impeccable breeding. And no one can dispute the fact that our families are richer than most."

Now, at last, they'd come to a crucial difference between them. Lila swallowed back the bitter words that had haunted her all her life. *Nouveau riche.* Yes, their families were rich, but Lila's family wasn't *born* rich—as if Fowler money was somehow different. Lila couldn't count the times she'd been snubbed by the very crowd she should have belonged to, all because her father had earned his fortune rather than inheriting it. Bruce, on the other hand, had nothing to worry about. The Patmans had been in money since the beginning of time.

Lila could feel her brow furrow, and knowing how unattractive that could be—not to mention fearing the wrinkles it'd encourage in her future—she pushed the unpleasant thoughts from her mind and tried to relax. She didn't want Pepper to see her looking like a prune.

"What now?" Bruce asked. "Would you like to have a swim?"

"Not really. Let's just walk awhile and decide later." Lila wasn't in the mood to commit to doing anything with Bruce right now, especially not something that would completely wreck her hair. She'd been willing to play tennis; it was Bruce's passion, and he'd never set foot on the premises without playing. But Lila's present goal was to find Pepper and do whatever Pepper was doing.

Well, this must be my lucky day, she thought, seeing Pepper's tall, thin outline framed in the ornate double doors of the clubhouse.

"Oh, look, there's Pepper," Lila announced over her shoulder at Bruce. "Why don't we find out what she and Anderson are doing?"

Pepper Danforth stepped onto the wide stone terrace behind the club's sunroom as Lila approached. The sun glinted off her short, white-blond hair. She had the height, the slimness, and the walk of a high-fashion model. "Lila, dear. How marvelous to see you!" She put both heavily jeweled hands on Lila's arms in more of a brace than a hug and made a little pecking motion toward each cheek. "Kiss-kiss," she said. "I'm so glad you were both able to make it today. How was your game?"

"I whupped butt," Bruce crowed, winking at Lila. Just for the express purpose of annoying her, she was sure.

"Where's Anderson?" Lila asked, shading her eyes with her hand in a show of searching for Anderson Pettigrew, Pepper's boyfriend.

"Oh, he's running around here somewhere." Pepper waved her arm in a vague sweep. "He's probably still on the golf course, but we're supposed to meet for lunch at one on the Great Lawn. We were hoping the two of you might join us."

"We'd love to," Lila gushed. It was exactly what she'd hoped for.

"Oh, wait." Pepper cocked her head sideways and posed with a hand on each hip. "You're not VIPs, are you?" She sighed noisily. "Pardon my faux pas! I'd nearly forgotten that today is Thursday. The Great Lawn is reserved for VIPs on weekdays. Of course, Couples-Only members can go there on the weekends, but . . ." She shrugged as if the matter were out of her hands.

Lila glanced toward Bruce in panic.

"Well, an invitation is an invitation," Pepper declared. "What kind of hostess would I be to extend an offer and then withdraw it? I'll simply have to pull a few strings and get you in—as my guests, of course."

Lila beamed. "Do you think it'll be OK?"

"I'm certain of it—if *I* say so. After all, the junior president of the VIP Circle should have some privileges, don't you think?"

"Well, what're we waiting for?" Bruce said impatiently. "I'm starved."

"Shall we?" Pepper linked her arm through Lila's and pulled her along while Bruce followed.

The Great Lawn was a broad expanse of lush green grass thicker than shag carpeting. It was surrounded on three sides by a virtual wall of flowers and shrubs. On the fourth side sat a white Victorian gingerbread-trimmed gazebo with a panoramic view of the golf course behind it. White tables topped with colorful yellow-striped umbrellas were scattered in a seemingly haphazard manner, turning the lawn into a private dining area.

"Your table is ready, Miss Danforth," the maitre d' said, appearing as if from nowhere. He wore the crisp white slacks and green knit shirt that indicated this was a casual section of the club.

"I've already ordered for us," Pepper said as they were seated, "but since I have guests, please double everything."

"Yes, miss," he said. "Cold skewered shrimp with dill sauce, a tray of assorted sandwiches, fresh raw vegetables, and a pitcher of iced tea—for four. I'll have it right out."

"Sounds yummy." Lila glanced nervously at Bruce to make sure he didn't object. She knew he hated what was politely called "finger food." Except for the occasional pizza or burger when he was slumming, he was strictly a steak-and-potatoes man.

He smiled back at her, rolling his eyes comically when Pepper looked the other way.

Lila gave him a look of warning and turned quickly back to Pepper, not wanting to encourage him. But judging from the expression of anger on Pepper's face, she was momentarily afraid Pepper had noticed Bruce's antics. "What's wrong?" Lila asked anxiously.

"This is a *perfect* example of what I was telling Anderson about just last night. The help we are getting at the club lately is *abominable*. I can't abide incompetence," Pepper said.

Lila tried to hide her bewilderment, but Pepper must have recognized the look of confusion on her face.

"Here, let me show you," she explained. "This umbrella isn't doing a bit of good. The sun is shining right on my arm." She waved her hand, motioning for the waiter to return. "It's absurd that I should have to point out things like that. He should have seen that the umbrella was all wrong and adjusted it before we sat down."

"I can do it," Bruce offered. He stood up, but Pepper stared him back into his seat.

"Our *waiter* can do it," Pepper snapped. "It's his job, after all!"

"Of course it is," Lila agreed before flashing

Bruce a look of annoyance. "Bruce, don't be silly!"

"Pardon me for being polite," Bruce whispered to Lila while Pepper was preoccupied with summoning a waiter.

A young waiter scurried to the table with the food, followed by a younger busboy bearing crystal water goblets, silverware, and china. The job fell on him to adjust the umbrella to Pepper's liking.

Lila opened her mouth to thank him, but when she saw that Pepper was going to say nothing, she kept quiet.

When the waiter uncovered the last dish and started to leave, Pepper caught him by the shirt, pulling his shirttail out in the process. "Ex-*cuse* me," she said rudely. "But you are going to have to take these sandwiches back. They're totally unacceptable." She turned up her nose as if there were bugs crawling on the food. "I distinctly asked that the sandwiches be cut in quarters, not halves."

The waiter patiently scooped up the silver tray. "Sorry, Miss Danforth. I must have misunderstood. I'll bring you fresh ones immediately."

"Some people!" Pepper griped before the waiter was out of hearing distance. But in the blink of an eye the smile returned to her face. She reached across the table and laid a hand on Lila's wrist. "Lila, I just heard the most interesting tidbit about you the other day, and I simply *must* know if it's true. Did you really open a doughnut shop that catered to the homeless?"

Lila's eyes bulged and her mouth opened awkwardly in ill-concealed shock, but she was rescued from having to answer by the arrival of Anderson Pettigrew. His hideous plaid pants and mauve shirt verified that he'd just come from the golf course.

"Hello, folks." He pulled off his sun visor and kissed Pepper on top of her head. "Why wasn't I told they were opening the Great Lawn to *everyone* today?"

A shiver of excitement ran up Elizabeth's spine the moment she walked into the office of the *Sweet Valley Gazette.* The huge crowded room was alive with the commotion of a newspaper being pulled together. The sounds of ringing phones, clacking computer keys, muted whispers, and shuffling papers, accompanied by the buzz of the fluorescent lights overhead, all blended into a familiar symphony that was music to her ears.

I'm home, she told herself. All the feelings she remembered from her years of work on her high-school newspaper, the *Oracle,* returned to her. She loved the familiar, busy look of the office, even the familiar scents. Although she knew the paper would be taken downtown for its final printing, she could almost smell the paper and ink.

A large guy who looked as if he'd have been more at home on a football field than in a newspaper office elbowed his way past them, sending Elizabeth slightly off-balance. Scott put his hands on her arms to steady her.

"Wow," she breathed, stepping out of his grasp. "You weren't kidding about not having much room, were you?"

Nearly every inch of floor space was covered with desks, tables, chairs, and filing cabinets. And nearly every inch of the space atop the office furniture was cluttered with papers, books, computer terminals, phones, faxes, and assorted office supplies.

"You can't say you weren't warned, so it's too late to change your mind."

"I have no intention of changing my mind. You're stuck with me now. Like it or not."

"Believe me, I like it." Scott grinned mischievously, but before she could comment, he turned and nudged her farther into the room. "Hey, everybody," he announced, "this is Elizabeth Wakefield, our new reporter."

A few hands flew up, and a few "Hello, Elizabeth"s floated back across the crowded office, but no one stopped what they were doing.

She glanced over the shoulder of a nearby reporter's computer screen and saw words being shaped into a story. *Now this is real writing. This is where I belong.*

She could hardly believe she was working on a newspaper again. Remembering how much working at the *Oracle* had meant to her during her high-school days, she couldn't imagine why she'd stayed away from newspaper journalism so long.

Of course I can, she reminded herself. *Two words: Tom Watts.* It annoyed her to think how she had let her personal life cloud her professional judgment for so long. Somehow her dreams of a future in journalism and her dreams of a future with Tom had become all entwined. After a while it'd become impossible to tell where one ended and the other began. She couldn't afford to be sidetracked any longer. She vowed to keep a clear head from here on out and never be swayed from her goals again.

The same guy who'd elbowed past them earlier returned from the opposite direction. "Get outta the door, Sinclair," he grumbled, shoving Scott's body against Elizabeth's. But to Elizabeth, he mumbled a semipolite, "Excuse me."

Elizabeth raised a disapproving eyebrow. "Nice guy," she remarked lightly.

Scott smirked as he led Elizabeth away from the direct path of traffic over to an empty spot near the copy machine.

She smiled teasingly. "Weren't you saying something on the way over here about how I'd appreciate the genteel pace of newspaper journalism as compared to the hectic pace at the TV station?"

Scott shrugged. "Well, it's usually not quite

this bad. But the deadline for the weekend edition is one o'clock today."

"That's right, Sinclair," a wiry guy agreed, hurrying past. "And that happens to be less than three hours from now. Do you have that profile story finished on the new biology professor?" He didn't wait for an answer. "Then get it on my desk, pronto."

"Ed," Scott called after him. "Ed, wait up. Here's someone I want you to meet." He turned to Elizabeth. "Are you ready to meet the editor?" he whispered.

"As ready as I'll ever be."

With Scott pulling her along by one arm, Elizabeth was off, threading her way between desks and tables, trying to catch the harried editor. They caught up to him in the doorway of his office.

Ed Greyson was the editor of the *Sweet Valley Gazette*. And although he was only a college senior, Elizabeth could almost picture him as a stereotypical crusty veteran newspaper editor in a few years. He was probably an inch or two shorter than she was, with a thatch of unruly brown hair. His thin lips made his square jaw seem even squarer, and the lenses of the little round wire-rimmed glasses perched atop his nose were so thick, they hid the color of his eyes.

"Welcome aboard, Elizabeth," he said when they were introduced. "Scott has been talking about you for weeks. According to him, you're just a slightly less important journalist than either Woodward or Bernstein."

"Thanks. I'll try to live up to my reputation."

"I'm sure you will, but we'll have to talk more about it later, OK? I don't mean to be unfriendly, but I'm really pressed for time right now. Why don't you let Scott show you where to park your gear and help you get you settled in?"

Before Elizabeth had time to comment, Ed disappeared into the office and the door shut practically in her face.

"He's a nice guy when you get to know him," Scott assured her. "He can be a total perfectionist and a bit of a slave driver at times, but you'll like him. C'mon, I'll show you your desk."

Scott led her to a medium-size desk right smack in the middle of the crowded room. While it wasn't quite what she'd hoped for, she tried not to let the disappointment show on her face. *Except for the lack of privacy, it's not so bad,* she assured herself. *Besides, what did you expect? You're the new kid. You're just used to being spoiled by working at WSVU. Everyone starts at ground level. It's up to you whether you climb or stay there. It won't be the first time you've had to prove yourself in a new situation.*

"This is great," she exclaimed, working up enough enthusiasm to sound convincing.

"I'm afraid you're going to have to share this desk with me," he apologized. "But hey, I'm flexible. I can work anywhere. Whenever you need the space, it's all yours."

She covered her surprise. "It'll be fine, Scott. I just hope I'm not inconveniencing you."

"Not a bit. What's mine is yours. I've cleared out the two drawers on the left for you, but I can make more room if you need it."

"Thanks. But two for you and two for me seems a pretty equitable solution." She began to pull items from her cardboard box and place them in the empty drawers. Picking up her flowered blotter and the matching mug, she decided they wouldn't look quite right on Scott's desk and shoved them back into the box. "I think I'll take most of this stuff back to the dorm with me."

Suddenly Ed dashed by their desk like a whirlwind. "Jeremy," he shouted to the heavyset guy who'd nearly run them over twice. "I just got a report that five students in Peterson Hall got food poisoning from the cafeteria's sausage burritos. Check it out."

"When do you want it?"

"Yesterday."

"Yeah, right. No rush. I'm on my way." Jeremy grabbed his backpack and was out the door in a blur.

Remembering the thrill of chasing a story, Elizabeth shivered. Her slight disappointment with the crowded conditions evaporated. She didn't care if she had to write out of the phone

111

booth in the hall. She was a newspaper reporter again, and she couldn't wait to get her first story. "Let's get started," she said to Scott with an excited smile.

"I know you're going to like it here, Liz," Scott assured her once again. He gave her a companionable one-armed hug.

This is perfect, Elizabeth thought. *Excitement, unlimited potential for advancement, and best of all, encouraging coworkers!*

Late Thursday afternoon Nick found himself once again sitting on a straight-backed chair in front of Chief Wallace's desk. He was tired. He'd been working all day trying to finish paperwork on three old cases, but at the same time he had a familiar burning in the pit of his stomach that always came with the desire to get started on a new case. Once his curiosity was aroused, he didn't like to wait around.

Chief Wallace paced another circle around his desk. He gestured with his unlit cigar as he filled Nick in on a couple of new developments in the Verona Springs murder. Since much of what he said was a repetition of what he'd said the day before, Nick was beginning to get the idea that the chief was stalling for some reason. His suspicions were confirmed when there was a tap at the door and a tall young woman with a short, red bob entered.

"Come on in, Eileen," Chief Wallace urged. "We've been waiting for you. Nick, this is Detective Eileen Rogers. She's just been transferred to our precinct."

Nick half stood, but she waved him back into his seat and flashed a gorgeous smile. "Glad to meet you, Detective Rogers," he said.

"I think you'd better call me Eileen." She grinned as if she knew something he didn't.

"Nick," Chief Wallace explained, "Eileen is your new partner."

"What?" Nick tried not to let the surprise show on his face. "I—I mean, what happened to Bill?"

"Nothing has happened to Bill, but I don't think he'd look as good in an evening gown, do you?"

Nick ran a hand nervously through his hair. He'd learned long ago that there was no rushing Chief Wallace. The chief would say what he wanted to say when he got good and ready to say it. Nick leaned back and prepared himself for the eventual explanation, but he had a distinct feeling deep in his gut that he wasn't going to like it.

Eileen dragged a chair over beside Nick and sat down. Up close he could see the sprinkling of copper freckles across her nose. She looked young—too young to be a detective. But then again, so did he. She crossed her long, shapely legs and leaned confidently toward Chief Wallace as he began to speak.

"On further investigation, Nick, it seems that just getting you into the Verona Springs Country Club isn't going to be enough. Apparently the real problems are deep within the inner circle of members, and it would be impossible for a single young man to infiltrate this circle. We suspect our answers lie in an area called the Couples-Only section of the club. And that's why we've brought in Eileen." Chief Wallace crossed his hairy arms and half sat, half leaned on the corner of his desk. "She's going undercover with you. As your girlfriend."

Nick looked at Eileen's confident smile and sparkling, golden brown eyes. *Uh-oh,* he thought. *Jessica is* not *going to like this.* Regardless, he kept a professional expression on his face and asked, "When do we start?"

"Tomorrow night. I've arranged for you to have dinner at Tucci's with Judge Harland Pettigrew. Pettigrew is a retired judge with more money than the mint. His family was instrumental in the founding of Verona Springs, but he's very unhappy with it nowadays. He says that over the past few years the management has been so busy catering to a younger, hipper crowd, the older members seem to have gotten lost in the shuffle. He and his friends rarely go there anymore. It could just be the ramblings of a dissatisfied old man, but it gave him enough incentive to want to cooperate with us."

"Can we trust him?" Nick crossed his arms over his chest.

"Implicitly. I've known Judge Pettigrew for years. He's honest, caring, and above all, trustworthy."

"How is he going to help?"

"He wants to meet you at dinner Friday night. If he thinks you'll pass muster with these people at the club, he plans to put you up for membership, claiming that you're the grandson of his wife's college roommate."

Nick glanced at Eileen, who seemed to taking in every word. "But what if the wife—"

"No danger in that. Priscilla Pettigrew died two years ago. And believe me, no one will think it's unusual for the judge to care about someone from his wife's past. It's common knowledge that he worshiped her. He's always doing something in honor of her memory."

"What about others who might have known Mrs. Pettigrew? Someone who might have known her from school, like the real ex-roommate?"

"Mrs. Pettigrew went to school back east somewhere, but I don't think you'd have to worry about that anyway. She graduated in the forties, and most of the Verona Springs crowd is young. That's why we need a young couple like you and Eileen. And as far as relatives go, his only son and daughter-in-law live in Boston and only visit at Christmas, so they shouldn't be a problem. I don't think the judge has any relatives in the state except a grandson."

Nick lifted a questioning eyebrow, which the chief immediately picked up on.

"Apparently the grandson has been living with the judge until recently. I don't think he'll pose any problems. In fact, I get the impression the main reason Pettigrew is going along with us on this is because he's worried about the guy."

Nick nodded confidently. Chief Wallace had never let him down on a background check yet.

"But there's one point I need to stress to both of you," the chief added. "On this job you'll have to remember you're a couple, so be sure to play up that angle. Stay together, hold hands, give each other those goofy, lovesick looks. You young people know what I mean. You have to convince these blue bloods you're perfect candidates for the Couples-Only section of the club."

"I think we can handle it," Eileen said, giving Nick's hand a quick pat.

"I know you can," the chief agreed without hesitation, turning to Eileen. "I have the utmost faith in Nick. He's one of my best officers. And as for you, Miss Rogers, I've studied your file. Chief Henderson has nothing but good things to say about your work. We're honored to have you working here."

"Thank you, sir." Eileen held out her delicate-looking hand, which practically disappeared in the chief's big paw as he shook it. Then she turned to Nick. "I'm staying at the Bayside Motel until I can find a new apartment. Will you pick me up tomorrow night, or do you want me to drive?"

"I think I'd better pick you up."

Eileen winked flirtatiously. "OK, it's a date. See you at eight."

"See you," Nick replied, trying to hold back the nausea in the pit of his stomach. Jessica was not going to like this *at all!*

Chapter Six

"You don't say?" Bruce said for what seemed like the fifteenth time. He blinked his long black lashes to try to stay awake. He'd long ago lost track of whether Pepper was talking about her personal trainer, her therapist, her chef, or the prince she'd met in the south of France. But it didn't matter since nothing she had to say was of any interest to him.

As she chattered on and on, he amused himself by watching the puddle of condensation collect around his frosty glass of iced tea. Pepper was as shallow as the puddle and twice as transparent. From her platinum hair to her painted toenails, she was as fake as the IDs most of his fraternity brothers used at bars.

He doubted there was an inch of her body that hadn't been nipped, tucked, or added to. He was certain her petite little upturned nose was the result of two factors: a surgeon's scalpel and long years of practicing the art of looking down it at other people.

And her boyfriend, Anderson Pettigrew, wasn't much better. From the moment he'd arrived at the table, he'd annoyed Bruce with his lord-of-the-manor air. Now he slouched lazily in his chair, nodding in all the right places at Pepper's monologue. What a pair!

But when Bruce glanced across the table and watched the light dance in Lila's brown eyes, he smiled. It was well worth every minute of boring conversation to see her happy. He hadn't seen her so animated in a long time.

Bruce had dated so many women he couldn't even remember them all, but he knew without a doubt that Lila Fowler was the most elegant, beautiful woman he had ever dated. And she had a lot more going for her than just surface beauty. She had impeccable manners, a quick wit, and most of all, a sense of style and grace that could only come with good breeding.

The white-and-navy shorts outfit she was wearing was a perfect example. She looked as if she'd walked off the set of the movie *The Great Gatsby*. Very twenties, very chic, very sophisticated. Lila's ability to achieve an understated elegance was beyond compare. She was so composed and natural, she looked as if she'd been born here.

Bruce loved her sense of style. He loved her looks. He just plain loved Lila Fowler. And he loved making her happy. His new philosophy of life was very simple: When Lila was happy, he was happy. He smiled grandly at Pepper just to prove the point. But his smile quickly faded as she once again showed her true colors.

"Leave the pitcher," Pepper brayed at the bus-boy who was refilling their nearly full water glasses. "I can't stand the help hanging over the table every minute!"

Bruce couldn't believe how rude she was. A quick glance in Lila's direction told him that it was bothering her too.

Apparently Pepper's story had ended. She took a sip of iced tea and reached for a plump shrimp. Like any good tag-team partner, Anderson jumped right into the fray of momentary silence with a boring story about nearly winning the club's pro-am golf tournament last year.

Suddenly Pepper shrieked. "Ugh! This shrimp is positively mushy. Why didn't one of you say something?" She grabbed Anderson's arm. "Come with me, Anderson. We're going to have a little talk with the chef."

"Pepper is by far the rudest person I've ever met," Bruce whispered to Lila after Pepper and Anderson had stalked out of hearing range. "She treats the help like animals."

"More like things," Lila said with disdain. "If animals were treated that way, someone would call the SPCA."

"I don't like her, Li."

"So? You don't have to like her. Just be nice to her."

"I don't know how much longer I can do that. I've already been tempted to cram a mushy shrimp—"

"Bruce Patman, I mean it. Pepper may be rude to some people, but she's been positively charming to us. Besides, she is absolutely the key for getting us into the VIP Circle. I just know it."

Lila's eyes sparkled as tears started to well up. Bruce could feel his resistance melting. He couldn't bear to see Lila cry. His heart had practically broken yesterday when he'd seen her sobbing for her lost husband. "OK, sweetheart," he promised. "I'll be nice to her, but remind me to leave the waiter a big tip. The poor guy's earned it."

"Shhh—here they come."

Both Lila and Bruce smiled and nodded their way through Pepper's account of telling off the chef.

At long last Bruce understood why his parents and Lila's parents had always insisted they go to public schools and hang out with "regular" kids. Although he knew he was far from average, he considered himself to be a nice enough guy. So what if he'd gone through a time in his adolescence when he was a bit unbearable with the money thing? All kids brag. But he thanked his lucky stars that he'd outgrown it. He'd hate to think that he might've turned out to be a jerk like Anderson Pettigrew. And he gave double thanks that his lovely Lila would never be anything like Pepper Danforth.

Suddenly a movement across the lawn caught Bruce's eye. A painfully thin young woman was flitting from table to table. She had her back to him, but something about her prissy, head-high walk was vaguely familiar. Then she turned, and he caught a glimpse of her profile. . . . *Oh no—Bunny Sterling!* He nearly spilled his iced tea.

"What's wrong with you, Bruce?" Lila hissed.

"Nothing," he choked out. He grabbed up his glass and began to gulp the ice-cold tea. He could tell by the look on Lila's face that he was embarrassing her, so he set down his glass. But he needed to hide behind something quickly. He scooted his chair over so that the table's tall floral centerpiece kept him out of Bunny's view.

"Shall I have the waiter come back and adjust the umbrella?" Pepper asked solicitously.

"No, thanks. I just wanted to sit closer to Lila."

He peeked again through the flowers. It was Bunny, all right. No one else had that big a head on that skinny a body. He knew why she was so thin—she never ate anything more fattening than carrot sticks. But he couldn't figure out why her head was so big. It certainly wasn't because it was loaded with brains. Bunny Sterling could be the poster girl for Airheads Anonymous. Not only was she silly, but she was impossibly vain. Her apparent purpose in life was to be a coat hanger for displaying garish designer fashions and gaudy jewelry.

Bunny was a society girl his fraternity brother Joey Timberlake had fixed him up with the previous summer. From the moment he'd picked her up, the date had gone badly. She was the blind date to end all blind dates. If she wasn't complaining, she was bragging about her father, a movie producer. She'd been such an utter bore that Bruce had sneaked out in the middle of the party, leaving her sitting in the hallway of the fraternity house, holding an empty bottle of wine.

That should have been the end of it, but it wasn't. Bunny had called him the next day to see how he was feeling. Evidently his friends had covered for him by telling her that he'd had too much to drink and had gotten sick. He'd assured Bunny that he was fine except for a slight hangover and thanked her for calling. He'd been cool about it—even distant—but that still wasn't the end. Bunny had called him again . . . and again. Seven or eight times a day for a whole week. She'd even memorized his schedule and started showing up at the fraternity house to walk him to classes.

Over the next couple of weeks Bruce could have written a book called *100 Unsuccessful Ways to Ditch a Girl*. He'd tried ignoring her, insulting her, making her jealous, telling her that he didn't want to be tied down, saying he'd return her calls and then not doing it. He tried everything he could think of until finally he'd had to resort to telling her the truth—flat-out—that she was dull and brainless, and he didn't want to see her again ever. She'd thrown a tantrum right in front of Sigma house. He hadn't minded paying for the window she'd thrown a rock through, but it took him weeks to get over the embarrassed stares of the crowd that had gathered to watch Bunny's ranting.

Bruce had no doubts that Bunny Sterling hated him. At the time it'd seemed like a worthwhile price to pay for getting rid of her. But now it could mean social suicide for both him *and* Lila if Bunny opened her big, toothy mouth.

Bruce's throat tightened. *And now she's headed straight for our table!* He grabbed Lila's arm more harshly than he'd intended.

"What?" Lila blurted, yanking her arm free. Her brown eyes flashed with extreme annoyance.

"Aren't you about ready to go?" Bruce suggested.

"Of *course* not. Pepper and I are having a *very* nice conversation. Why don't you behave and talk to Anderson?"

"Please, Li, I'm not feeling too well. Maybe it was the mushy shrimp. You know how delicate my palate is."

For a moment Bruce got the impression Lila

was going to totally ignore his discomfort, but suddenly Pepper, of all people, came to his rescue.

"He does look a little green around the gills, Lila. I *knew* those shrimp were bad. You just wait. *Some*-body is going to hear about this."

Despite his gratitude for Pepper's concerned intervention, Bruce felt a sudden pang of remorse that he was probably getting the chef into more trouble. "Well, maybe it wasn't the shrimp, but—"

"Nonsense. Don't you worry about a thing. I'll see that things are rectified pronto." Pepper turned to Lila. "You should take him home and put him to bed. I'm sure he'll be better by tomorrow, and we can just continue our visit then."

Lila took Bruce's arm and helped him from his chair. The stomachache story was even better than he'd originally planned. It gave him a reason to stay hunched over, head down, until they were well away from the Great Lawn *and* the creepy Bunny Sterling.

Back up a little, Elizabeth pleaded. She was leaning so closely toward the computer screen that she could feel the little tingles of static electricity it gave off. Any closer and she would probably mash her nose. But Scott was so close behind her that she could actually feel his breath on the back of her neck. She shivered involuntarily and wished that for once she'd worn her hair down instead of up in its customary casual ponytail. True, it was awfully close quarters in the *Gazette* office, but hadn't Scott ever heard of personal space?

Scott edged forward even more until his chin-length blond hair brushed her ear. "All you have to do is type in research, slash, dot, dot, city desk. . . ." He reached around her with both arms and put his hands on the keyboard. "Here. Want me to—"

"I think I remember how to type, Scott," she interrupted, shrugging his arms away. But seeing the injured look in his eyes, she immediately regretted her tone. "Sorry. First-day nerves, I guess."

He smiled down at her. "That's OK. But I don't know why you'd be nervous. You have talent, experience, and an unbelievable sense of news. You're a born newspaper reporter."

"Thanks," she replied, nudging him away as subtly as she could. "I just hope I remember how to write a newspaper story."

"Of course you will. No one could forget that. And don't worry about this computer system. I know you'll easily catch on to it. Even though it's the most up-to-date setup available, it's really a pretty straightforward program." He clicked the mouse pointer to shut down the terminal. "I have faith in you."

"That's sweet," she said. "Your confidence means a lot to me because frankly I'm worried that I might have trouble switching back. I was at the station so long that the way we did things there has become almost automatic."

"You won't have any trouble. Trust me. I know what I'm talking about. Before you know it, all traces of those sloppy WSVU methods will be washed cleanly from your mind."

Elizabeth blushed. She enjoyed Scott's enthusiasm, and at this point in her life, when her self-assurance was at an all-time low, she could certainly use a little praise. But at the same time she wished he wouldn't keep belittling the TV station. She had done some very good work there—work she was proud of.

"Oh, great. I can see it in those aqua eyes; I've done it again," Scott said. He leaned so close, she could see a few faint blond whiskers on his chin.

He needs a shave, Elizabeth realized, momentarily distracted.

"I don't mean to put down WSVU, and I sure didn't mean to imply you didn't do a good job there. You know I didn't. I'm your number-one fan. I used to watch the campus news every Tuesday and Thursday night just to see you. When you broke that story about the point-shaving scandal, you became my hero. And that exposé you did about sexual harassment at Kitty's Restaurant—that was major reporting."

"Whew," she said, fanning her hands to cool her blushing cheeks. "I don't know what to say. You're sure making it tough on me. How's a girl supposed to live up to such lofty expectations?"

"If anyone can do it, you can," he replied.

As Elizabeth self-consciously fumbled for her purse she thought, *Everyone likes a compliment now and then, but isn't Scott Sinclair overdoing it just a bit?*

"Hey, Jess!" Jessica heard as she entered the police station. She turned to see a uniformed officer she'd met during her last visit leading a handcuffed prisoner toward the holding cells.

"Hi, Luke," Jessica replied with a casual wave. She loved coming to the police station. Everyone was always so friendly and helpful, it was like visiting a big happy family. But most of all she loved the buzz of energy and excitement that surrounded the place. Everyone seemed to be doing something important every minute of the day. She could almost feel the vibration of anticipation in the air, as if something—anything—could happen at any moment. As if to illustrate her thoughts, two plainclothes officers dashed past her. One was buckling on a shoulder holster while the other fumbled with a bulletproof vest.

One of these days, she thought, *I'll be a real part of all this. They'll all think of me as Nick's partner instead of his girlfriend.*

As she turned the corner and started down the hall toward the detectives' office she heard a loud wolf whistle. She grinned, knowing the source immediately. It had to be Dub Harrison.

Someone who didn't know he was a chronic kidder might get offended by his antics, but Jessica knew it was only his way of trying to make her feel welcome. Although he was forever pretending to be a mean, tough cop, he was really a big, funny teddy bear. She couldn't help but like him.

Ever since she'd met Dub, he'd made it a game to always have some crazy little name to call her. If she wasn't Nick's Chick, she was the Sorority Babe or Nick's Late Date. But today, thanks to the poster she'd seen at the Mug Shot, she was ready with a comeback.

"Hey, Beach Blonde," he joked. "What's up?"

"Not much, Rub-a-dub Dub. Where's your tub?"

Dub's neck and ears turned scarlet, but he didn't miss a beat. "Watch it. You're going to have to start paying rent if you hang around here much more."

"You wish! You're going to have to start paying *me* for the privilege of letting you feast your eyes on my beauty."

He laughed. "You got me there, but don't expect much on a policeman's pay. What's in the sack? A present for me?"

"It's for Nick. I'm just dropping by to surprise him with some decent food. It's a turkey sandwich from the deli. He said he'd be in his office all day."

"Want me to give it to him? I'm headed that way; it'll save you the trip."

She knew that he knew very well she wanted to see Nick and that the sandwich was just a good excuse to drop in and spend a little time at the station. "No, thanks," she said with a grin. "I think he'd rather have a delivery from my own hands."

"No doubt," Dub said with a chuckle. "But actually he's in with the chief right now. Come on in and wait at his desk."

"That's OK. I'll just wait out here in the hall." *That way I can see him sooner,* she thought. *Maybe I can grab a kiss or two without Nick's coworkers as an audience.*

Dub had hardly had time to shut the door of the detectives' room when the door to Chief Wallace's office opened. Jessica rushed forward to meet Nick, but to her surprise, an aristocratic-looking, slender, elegant woman with short, copper red hair stepped into the hallway. Jessica nearly crashed right into her.

Before Jessica could apologize for her clumsiness, Nick appeared behind the redhead. *Very close* behind.

"Jessica!" Nick stepped back in surprise, but before he had time to say another word, Chief Wallace's voice came booming from behind the door.

"You two lovebirds have fun tomorrow night, but keep your eyes and ears open," he called out.

131

Lovebirds? Jessica's whole body tensed. She looked from Nick's startled face to the woman's calm smile. "Have I come at a bad time?" she asked in a voice an octave higher than usual.

"Oh, man, I knew this was going to happen." Nick groaned, running a hand roughly over his face. He closed his cool green eyes for a moment before meeting her gaze head-on. "It's not what you're thinking, Jess."

"Oh? And what am I thinking?" She stuck a hand at her hip, lifted her chin defiantly, and glared.

"This is Eileen. I mean, Detective Eileen Rogers."

Jessica forced a smile and a curt nod at the shapely redhead as she positioned herself between Nick and the other woman.

"I'm Nick's new partner," Eileen said in a whispery, Marilyn Monroe voice.

Jessica set her glare to *kill*.

Nick gulped loudly and tugged at the collar of his shirt. "Eileen and I are going to be working together. She and I have an assignment, under-cover—"

"I'll just bet you do!" Jessica interrupted. "Exactly what kind of covers do you two plan to be under?"

"Very funny. You know better than that. This is strictly business—"

132

"Don't talk to me. I'm not quite as bubble-headed as you seem to think I am."

"Jessica, calm down and let me explain."

"No. Don't bother explaining. I understand perfectly. *She's* good enough for you to take on a stakeout, but I'm *not!*" She threw the lunch sack more at him than to him before storming down the hall and out the station door.

Chapter Seven

_____

If I didn't know better, I'd think I was in the wrong place, Elizabeth thought as she stepped into the *Gazette* office Friday morning. Yesterday's madhouse had turned into today's tomb. It was still as crowded with furniture as an overstocked warehouse, but there wasn't a soul in sight. Not even Scott, and he was the one who'd left the message on her answering machine that she should stop by on her way to class.

Elizabeth walked over to the desk she and Scott shared. There on the computer screen was a bright yellow sticky note that read simply, "See me. Ed." She peeled the note from the screen. Did it mean "Elizabeth, see me," or "Scott, see me"?

"Well, there's only one way to find out," she murmured. As she hurried across the room to Ed Greyson's office, praying the message was for her,

her whole body trembled with anticipation. *This is it!* she thought excitedly. *I'm back in the newspaper game. I'm about to get my first assignment!*

The door to Ed's office stood open, so Elizabeth tapped lightly on the doorframe.

"Enter," Ed called out before looking up. "Oh, hi, Elizabeth. I'm surprised you're here so bright and early on a Friday morning." In faded jeans and an old, ratty sweatshirt he looked more like a college student and much more approachable than he had the day before. Still, she approached timidly.

"Did you want to see me?" she asked, holding up the sticky note.

"No, I left that note for the other Elizabeth Wakefield!" he said sarcastically, waving her inside. "Of course I want to see you. Clear off a chair and have a seat. I have your first assignment, if you think you're ready for it."

"What's the story?" she asked, trying not to sound as excited as she felt.

"I want you to go out to the Verona Springs Country Club and meet with a woman named Pepper Danforth. The club is sponsoring a big charity tennis bash next week, and they want some pre-event publicity."

"Oh." Elizabeth's mouth went dry. *Great,* she thought, hoping she was hiding her disappointment. *I'm getting the society page. Maybe he'll let me do recipes next.* She mentally kicked herself for getting her hopes up so high; the sudden fall was like a drop down the elevator shaft of a skyscraper.

"It's no big deal," Ed continued. "Just the usual who, what, and when. Think you can handle it?"

Elizabeth bristled. Not only was this going to be a boring assignment, but he was also insulting her by reminding her of the most elementary basics of journalism. "What about the where, why, and how?" she sneered, finishing off the list of story questions she'd learned back in grade school.

Ed pushed his glasses up his nose and stared. Elizabeth averted her eyes, horrified that she'd probably just blown her chance with this new editor. *He's going to think I'm impossible to work with. Why didn't I keep my big mouth shut?* she scolded herself.

"By all means include the where," he said at last. "But you'll be hard-pressed to come up with a why. It's beyond plain mortals like you and me to understand why that snooty bunch does anything. Just be sure you spell everyone's name correctly. Those society types are picky about that sort of thing."

Elizabeth's mouth dropped open. He was treating her as if she'd never even *read* a newspaper. This assignment was so basic, Jessica could have done it. And *she* hated writing anything longer than her signature across the bottom of a charge card slip.

Maybe I'll just pass it on to her, Elizabeth

thought. *She'd love to hang out at a country club and write about who was with whom and what they were wearing. She'd certainly fit in a lot better than I would.*

Elizabeth had never liked country clubs or sororities. They were too cliquish. That was why she hadn't joined a sorority when she arrived at SVU, even though Jessica had dragged her to countless pledge parties. Even her mother, who'd been a Theta in her college years at SVU, didn't pressure Elizabeth to join the sorority where she'd have been welcomed with open arms.

"Insulted?"

"No." Elizabeth tried not to wince at the sound of her own unconvincing voice.

"Forgive me, Ms. Woodward-and-Bernstein. I'm sorry that I couldn't offer you Watergate."

"I'm not after Watergate. I just don't appreciate being treated like a beginner. I was the editor of my high-school paper, and I've been an intern at—"

"Elizabeth, this is a *college* paper. *Everyone* here was the editor of their high-school paper, or yearbook, or something."

"Maybe so, but—"

"OK," he said. "Forget it. Let's start over. Personally I don't blame you for being annoyed. I guess I was being a bit pompous a moment ago. It's a little jealousy chip I carry on my shoulder for broadcast journalists."

"I'm not a broadcast journalist—not anymore."

"Touché." He came around the desk and stood in front of her. "I suppose I might as well level with you."

Elizabeth crossed her legs and her arms but tilted her face—not much. He was too short to look up to.

"To be perfectly honest, this assignment has sort of been rammed down our throats. No one at the paper wanted it. You were the new kid, so . . ." He lifted both his hands in a helpless gesture. "Think of it as a puff piece that'll acclimate you to print journalism again."

"All right, Ed," she said, uncrossing her arms. "I apologize for overreacting. It was very unprofessional of me. As the new kid, I understand my place. I'll be happy to do the story."

Ed returned to his seat behind the desk. He somehow seemed taller there.

Elizabeth leaned forward. "But why are we doing it if you don't think it's a worthwhile story?"

"Three very good reasons. Number one: Dr. Drucker, our faculty sponsor, is a fanatic when it comes to tennis, and the Verona Springs Country Club always invites him and his wife to play in the tourney. Number two: We're obligated to the club for providing so many part-time jobs for SVU students who need work. And last, but not anywhere near least: Pepper Danforth's daddy gives big bundles of money to the college every year. Pepper seems to think that means the paper should act as her personal publicity agent." He handed Elizabeth a scrap of paper. "Here's Pepper's phone number. Call her and set up a time to meet."

Elizabeth skimmed the paper, folded it, and stuffed it into her jeans pocket as Ed continued.

"I know when I handed you the story, you were probably thinking a simple press release form could have done the job. Just call Pepper, ask a couple of questions, fill in a few blanks, type it up, and list it in the upcoming calendar of events. But that won't do at all. Pepper wants a reporter to come out to the club. She doesn't want a classified ad . . . she wants a *story*. And you can be sure she expects to be the star of the show."

"Are you telling me that I have to write a piece to please this Danforth woman? If you are, you'd better find yourself another flunky."

Ed smacked his hands together, and Elizabeth jumped. *Oh, now I've done it. All I was doing was trying to be honest and open with him, and I've made him so angry, he's probably going to tell me to go back to WSVU.*

However, when Ed removed his glasses, Elizabeth was surprised to see that he was laughing. His whole body shook, but he hardly made a sound.

"I knew you were going to be good for us," he

said, wiping his eyes. "I'm well aware of your scruples in reporting, Elizabeth. Scott Sinclair isn't the only person around here who's seen you on WSVU." He replaced his wire-rimmed glasses. "No, you write the story however you see fit. All we're obligated to do is send out a reporter. That's what Miss Danforth has demanded, and that's what we'll do."

"So you're saying that as long as I go out to the club and let Pepper Danforth show me around, you wouldn't be averse to letting me dig a little deeper?"

"I don't think you could dig too deep out there without hitting . . . uh, shall we say . . . fertilizer?"

"Maybe so, but I can do more than describe their tennis outfits. There could be all kinds of angles to a story out there. I could approach it from a psychological angle or even a personal interest angle. Why do these people sponsor charity events? Is it just for the tax write-off? Is it just an excuse to have a party? Or do they honestly care about a cause? What kind of people join country clubs? Why do they join clubs? Why do they exclude other people? I could get to know some of the members, and . . ."

"OK, OK." Ed chuckled. "I think maybe Pepper Danforth has met her match at long last. You cover the club from whatever angle you want. It's your story. But be forewarned, I still have final say on whether we run it or not."

"I know. You're the editor. But trust me, you'll want to print it. It's going to be great."

"One more thing," Ed added. "The Verona Springs Country Club has a tougher caste system than old India. Pepper spends all her time either in the VIP Circle or in the Couples-Only areas. Either way, you won't even be able to get your foot in the door without a date. Do you think your boyfriend would be willing to tag along?"

Boyfriend? Elizabeth felt suddenly nauseous. "I—I'm not dating anyone right now."

"Oh?" Ed tapped his pencil on his desk. "Well, I guess we have a little problem here. Do you have a friend who owes you a favor?"

"Maybe I can help," a familiar voice offered.

Elizabeth whirled around to see Scott peeking around the edge of the open door.

"Ah, yes, Sinclair. Maybe you can. Elizabeth needs an escort while she's covering a story at the Verona Springs Country Club. Would you care to apply for the job?"

"My pleasure." Scott hurried over to stand by her chair.

Despite the fact that Elizabeth appreciated Scott coming to the rescue, she felt a sudden inexplicable uneasiness. Quickly she talked herself out of it. *It never hurts to have a partner on a story—especially a journalist as experienced as Scott. But still . . .*

"You'd have to pretend to be her attentive, loving

soul mate—not just her note-taking assistant. Do you think you could carry that off?"

"No problem," Scott said, placing his hands on Elizabeth's shoulders. "No problem at all."

"Do you really mean it, Anthony?" Dana asked excitedly. "Do you really think I can do it?"

"I really, really mean it," Anthony Davidovic, Dana's cello tutor and orchestral music professor, said with a grin. "If you keep progressing at this rate, there's no doubt in my mind that you'll be the featured soloist in the spring concert. In fact, that was the best practice we've had all week."

Dana beamed. Those were the very words she'd been waiting to hear. She slipped her sheet music into her folder and snapped her cello case shut.

With a jangle of keys Anthony opened the storage closet and methodically poked his music into its proper pigeonhole. "I take it you and Tom have worked things out?"

"I think so," Dana replied without going into detail. Anthony seemed so genuinely concerned about his students' lives that it'd been easy for Dana to confide in him about her hot-cold boyfriend from the very start. But today she didn't want to elaborate—it might jinx everything.

"Well," Anthony said after a moment. "Anyway, I'm glad you were able to shake whatever's been bothering you and get your mind back on your music."

Dana nodded enthusiastically. "Is it OK if I lock this in your closet and pick it up later today?" she asked, barely able to conceal her happiness. "I have a lot of things to do on campus before going home, and I don't want to drag it around."

"Sure," he said, standing aside so she could set the heavy cello case against the wall. "Keep up the good work, though. Whatever it is that's put the passion back in your music, stick with it."

Oh, I plan to, she thought as she hurried out of the studio. *You can count on it.*

Dana hummed happily as she danced across the quad. It was amazing how a little pickup in the romance department made everything else in life go smoother. Today's tutoring session with Anthony had been her first decent practice since she'd had that little episode with a very grumpy Tom in the parking lot last week. It had been impossible to concentrate on the cello after Tom had not only broken their date but acted as if he didn't care if he ever saw her again.

But that was the past. Now that her love life was back on track, she was determined not to let it get derailed again. She had no intention of letting Tom forget what a wonderful person she was, even if she had to call him or stop by to remind him every day. She knew he liked her—when he was with her. All she had to do was make sure he kept his mind on her and didn't slip into brooding about Elizabeth Wakefield, the Wicked Witch of WSVU.

And since their date wasn't until Sunday, she'd decided now was as good a time as any to refreshen his memory a bit. Strike while the iron was hot and all that. She had a couple of hours to kill before her harmony and composition class; where better to spend that time than at the WSVU building with Tom? If she was lucky, maybe she could even lure him away from work to go have a cup of coffee. It would be good for them to be seen out together more. Maybe then people would quit connecting him with Elizabeth.

"Tom?" she sang out as she neared his office.

"In here," he called. "It's open!"

She peeked her head around the side of the door. There was Tom with his back to her—alone. He was bent over his desk, looking like a man waiting for a tax audit. Dana skipped into the room, the bracelet of jingle bells she wore around her ankle tinkling with every bouncy step. "Guess who!" she cried, covering his eyes with her hands.

"Tinkerbell?" he asked, straightening up. He peeled her hands from his eyes and looked at them without turning around. "Hmmm, no. It must be Dana Upshaw. The blue nail polish and cello calluses are a dead giveaway."

"Ta da! You win the prize."

"What prize is that?"

"Me, silly." She dropped into his lap and kicked her feet playfully.

"Lucky me." Tom gave her a brief kiss on the

tip of her nose but then dropped his teasing tone. "But really, Dana, I'm pretty busy here at the moment. I have all this work to do, and it seems we're a little shorthanded at the station right now."

Dana stumbled slightly as Tom deposited her unceremoniously back on her feet.

Shorthanded? She glanced toward Elizabeth's desk. It had been neatly bare the day she'd taken the letter from it, but today it looked different. It had more than just a gone-for-the-day look. The desk had a cleaned-out, lock-stock-and-barrel, gone-from-the-premises-forever kind of look. *Yes!* Dana cheered silently, restraining herself from doing a victory dance behind Tom's chair.

Had Tom finally seen the light and thrown Elizabeth out? Did they have a big, hairy, awful screaming fight? Dana hoped so. She hoped he'd thrown her out by her long blond ponytail. But while she was dying to know what'd really happened, she didn't dare ask. Why remind Tom of the very thing she wanted him to forget? Besides, Elizabeth was a very touchy subject with him. Just mentioning her name could bring out a very snarly side of Tom that Dana didn't want to see right now.

She tore her gaze from the vacant desk that used to be Elizabeth's space. "You should have heard me at practice today, sweetie," she said, hoping to recapture Tom's attention. "I was superb."

"Uh-huh," he mumbled, rolling his chair to

the file cabinet and pulling out a file.

"Tom? I just came over to tell you how excited I was about our date Sunday."

"Sunday?"

"To-om!" she whined in frustration.

"Oh yes. Sunday. The country club. It'll be great," he said absently.

Dana tugged the neckline of her tight stretchy top slightly lower and leaned flirtatiously against his desk. "What are you working on?"

"A story for tonight's broadcast."

"Want me to help?"

"Yes, I do. If you'd run along to class and let me get some work done, it'd be a great help."

Not on your life, Mr. Tom Watts. I'm not giving up that easily. She leaned closer. "Tommy?" she crooned inches from his ear. "Tom-Tom."

He looked up. "What, Dana?"

"Unclench your jaw. C'mon, do it for me." She ran a finger up his arm, across his shoulder, over his jaw, and lightly across his lips. "There are other ways I can help, if you'll quit ignoring me," she whispered, sliding back into his lap. She tickled the back of his ear with her finger.

"Comfortable?" he asked, grinning.

"Uh-huh, I'm getting that way." She nuzzled against his chest. "How about you?"

"Too comfortable," he said with a laugh. "But I really do need to get this work done."

"Go ahead. Don't mind me. I'll just sit right

here and watch." She traced her finger delicately around the collar of his shirt.

"Dana!"

"Can't you work with me sitting here?"

"I can't even *think* with you sitting there." He caught her teasing hand. "Especially if you won't sit still!"

Dana smiled triumphantly. Mission accomplished! "Well, OK, then," she purred. "If you'll be patient long enough for me to tell you why I stopped by, I'll go away and let you get back to your precious work."

"OK, I'm all ears."

"Oh no, you're not." She giggled. "But I'll tell you anyway." She ran her fingers through his hair. "First of all, I wanted to thank you again for inviting me to the Verona Springs Country Club."

"And second?" Tom asked.

"I wanted to remind you of something."

"What?"

"This," Dana said. She pulled his face to hers and proceeded to give him a kiss that he'd be lucky to recover from by Sunday.

By the time she unwound her arms from his neck, he didn't seem quite so anxious to rush her away. So for her final act she stood up, straightened her skirt, and walked to the door. Her job was done—for now.

"Tom," she said, pausing in the doorway.

"What, Dana?" he asked with a wicked grin.

"Hurry and get all this work done. I want your schedule perfectly free by Sunday. I want you all to myself—no distractions."

"No distractions," he repeated. "Just you and me, I promise."

Just you and me / As it should be, Dana sang in her mind as he left the station. *Things are better / Since I stole the letter / Elizabeth's gone / And Tom's all alone—*

"Well, it almost rhymes," she muttered.

—and the field is wide open for me!

She laughed at her silly composition. *Maybe I'll go practice the cello for a while,* she told herself. *I think the passion in my music is about to jump off the Richter scale!*

We've been sitting here on the Great Lawn so long, the sun has moved, Bruce thought as he scooted his chair away from the direct ray of sunlight that was blinding him.

"Will you sit still!" Lila complained under her breath.

Right, Bruce thought. *You can gripe. The umbrella is shading you completely. I'm the one sitting here getting roasted.* He gave her what he hoped was a wilting look and scooted his chair once more for good measure. Finally settled in the shade of the yellow-striped umbrella, he turned his face back toward the gazebo, where a string quartet was screeching away.

It wasn't long, however, before the gazebo and its contents blurred into the foreground as Bruce stared longingly past them toward the lush, emerald greens of the golf course beyond. Even though he was a tennis man, he suddenly wished he'd invited a few of his fraternity brothers out for a game of golf. Right now, he was bored senseless.

"Bruce, sit still!" Lila demanded a little more loudly than she had the first three times. "You're fidgeting like a kindergartner in church."

"Don't tell me you're enjoying this insipid music, Lila. I can tell by the way you're struggling not to yawn that you just *adore* it."

"At least I'm trying to *look* interested. Can't you at least pretend?"

"It's hard to pretend every minute of the day."

"Don't start with me again, Bruce. I'm still mad at you."

Bruce sighed loudly. They had been fighting ever since breakfast, when he'd confided in her about Bunny. "Are you still mad at me about Bunny Sterling? You aren't, are you?"

Lila ignored him, but he could tell by the rapid tap, tap, tap of her perfectly manicured fingernails against the tabletop that she was still very much annoyed.

Well, no more than I am, he thought. And looking at those long pink nails annoyed him even further. She'd made him drive all the way into Los Angeles last night so she could go to

150

Pepper's favorite manicurist and get the exact shade of pink polish that Pepper wore. He couldn't remember the name of the absurd-looking lacquer, even though Lila had babbled about it all the way home. *It should have been called puke-medicine pink,* Bruce thought, stifling a laugh. *Maybe it looks OK on Pepper, but it's all wrong for Lila.*

Tap, tap, tap, tap . . . It was more annoying than the music. "You aren't jealous, are you?" he asked. "Because if that's what's bothering you, you can just forget it. I only had one date with Bunny, and it was way before you and I even started being civil to each other."

"I'm not jealous."

"Good. Because she meant nothing to me."

"You've already said that twice."

Bruce noticed that the people at the next table were starting to give them dirty looks. "Maybe so," he said, lowering his voice slightly, "but I still get the impression you don't believe me. She was a fix up. I only went out with her as a favor to Joey Timberlake. I didn't even stick out the whole date. Besides, I thought we agreed not to worry about each other's romantic past. *You* were the one who suggested we never pry into what was ancient history."

"Bruce, drop it. I couldn't care less about your old girlfriends. I saw you mess with girls' minds all through high school, so I know how you are." She picked up her champagne glass and drained it in

151

one gulp. "But couldn't you at least have had the foresight not to mess with someone so important to our social future?"

"Shhh," someone hissed from the next table.

Lila snapped her mouth shut and kicked Bruce under the table.

"Well, pardon me!" he said, leaning to rub his aching shin. "You're right, of course. How utterly stupid of me. I should have checked my crystal ball first."

Bruce dropped his voice to a low mutter when he realized Lila wasn't listening anyway. "I probably should have consulted the stars and formed a lasting alliance with her just in case a future girlfriend would want to use her back for social climbing. . . ."

Bruce trailed off when Lila turned toward the quartet and pasted on a fake half smile. He knew it was fake; he'd seen her practicing it all morning in front of the mirror.

Groaning, Bruce lifted his hand and flicked his fingers to get the waiter's attention. Once he'd made eye contact, he pointed toward his champagne glass. Immediately the waiter hurried to the table and refilled Bruce's glass.

Bruce downed the cold, bubbly liquid, all the while keeping a lookout for Bunny Sterling.

"You're drinking too much," Lila hissed when the waiter was gone. "And I wish you'd quit peering around like you expect someone to jump out of the bushes at us."

As Lila nagged, Bruce noticed Pepper heading their way with Anderson in tow.

He tapped Lila's arm and cut his glance toward the advancing couple. Lila immediately broke off her scolding and beamed with graciousness.

"Pepper! Anderson! Won't you join us?" she cooed. "We're having champagne to celebrate two whole weeks of membership here."

"To membership," Bruce toasted, tossing down the rest of his champagne.

"And to new friends," Lila added gaily as she lifted her glass.

Anderson pulled out a chair. Today he'd exchanged his Lord-of-the-Golf-Course look for casual chic. Bruce, who believed in looking impeccable at all times, felt Anderson had gone way overboard. His polo shirt was OK, but the slept-in khakis and the scuffed deck shoes were a bit much. "I can see you two are enjoying yourselves," he said grandly. "Wasn't it lovely of our Pepper to arrange special permission for you to lunch here on a VIP-only day?"

"Oh yes. We're having a marvelous time, as we always do here," Lila gushed.

"Simply marvelous," Bruce agreed. He realized he was wearing the same fake smile as Lila, but he wasn't about to wipe it off. He didn't want these people to think he wasn't VIP material. No Patman had ever been excluded from anything. He wasn't about to be the first.

"We were hoping that you two would be around today," Lila continued. "We do so enjoy your company. Don't we, sweetheart?"

"You bet," Bruce enthused as he flagged down a waiter for more champagne. "I was just saying to Lila a moment ago how I wished the two of you were here to share this lovely music with us."

Nick stepped out of the white classic Thunderbird, straightened his navy blazer, and handed the keys to the valet.

"Nice car, man," the valet said.

Nick handed him a generous tip. "Take good care of it."

"You bet."

"He'd better," Nick whispered to Eileen, "or you and I are toast."

"It was nice of Bill to lend you his car while we're on this case."

"Nice doesn't begin to cover it. For Bill, it was the supreme sacrifice. That Thunderbird is his pride and joy. He'd sooner put up one of his family members as a decoy in a sting operation than risk anything happening to his car."

"Did the chief make him do it?"

"No. Bill volunteered. But it's a good thing he did. I don't think we'd have made much of an impression in my Camaro, and although your Toyota might be a mother's dream come true, I doubt it would have turned any heads here with this bunch."

"Hey, don't dis my car."

"No, disrespect intended, ma'am."

"Not too much taken," she said with a laugh.

Eileen's laugh was gentle and controlled—sort of like Eileen herself. Nothing like Jessica's spontaneous, free-spirited laughter that he loved. Jessica . . . who hadn't spoken to him since she'd angrily stormed out of the police station the day before.

Nick stopped himself from planning how to get Jessica to listen to reason and took Eileen's arm. They entered the restaurant in a well-staged dating pose, just in case someone from the club was watching.

Tucci's was an Italian restaurant frequented by members of the Verona Springs Country Club. Beyond its etched glass doors lay a world of enticing sights and smells. Their own advertising summed it up as "an old-world dining experience." The deep maroon of the carpets and upholstery and the dark mahogany paneling, tables, and chairs were offset by brilliant green plants and bright floral arrangements.

Arm in arm, Nick and Eileen made their way across the crowded vestibule. The maitre d' stared blindly over their heads.

"We're Judge Pettigrew's party," Nick declared, cutting in line. Instantly the maitre d's attitude changed. He snapped his fingers at a nearby waiter.

As they followed the waiter through the crowded restaurant Nick noticed that Eileen was getting a lot of appreciative stares. He had to admit, she was an attractive woman. With those golden cat eyes and hair the color of a brand-new penny, she reminded him of an autumn bouquet— all browns, oranges, and greens. Tonight she was wearing a tasteful but elegant green dress that made her look older and more sophisticated than she had in the office the day before. "You look lovely tonight," he said.

"Thanks," she replied without the slightest trace of coyness or embarrassment. "It's nice to be able to wear something like this. My last under-cover job had me in a chartreuse Lycra miniskirt, black fishnets, and a hot pink lace bustier."

Nick lifted one eyebrow suggestively.

"Don't ask," she said with a laugh.

The waiter led them down a couple of steps to a ground-level, glassed-in room that was a virtual jungle of vines, potted plants, and trees. Judge Harlan Pettigrew was already seated at a table for six near the large windows overlooking the sparkling lights of the valley. The judge was a tall, muscular man who looked much younger than his seventy years. He had bushy white hair, thick white eyebrows, and sparkling clear blue eyes. Nick liked him immediately.

"Nick, my boy," the judge said as if they were long lost friends. He clasped Nick's hand between both of his. "I'm glad you could make it."

Nick introduced Eileen. Even though no one else was at the table, the judge seemed to want to keep up the pretense that Nick was his wife's roommate's grandson.

A waiter filled their wineglasses. While Eileen swirled the red liquid in her glass and talked comfortably with the judge about its bouquet, Nick inwardly scolded himself for not having done a little research on fine wines. He'd spent hours the night before reading about table etiquette, tennis rules, fashions, stocks, bonds, and real estate, but the wine thing had escaped him. He'd been working undercover with car thieves and drug dealers too long. Evidently he still had a few rough edges to polish before passing himself off as high society.

The waiter returned and set a wicker basket of bread on the table. "And what about young Mr. Pettigrew," he asked amiably. "Will he and Miss Danforth be joining you tonight?"

"No, Lorenzo. Not tonight."

"That was about my grandson," the judge explained after the waiter had gathered the extra place settings and hurried away. "Ordinarily he and his girlfriend join me for supper on Friday evenings, but lately it seems something always comes up that they consider to be more important. It usually has something to do with the club—that special group of theirs seems to be forever calling emergency meetings of some sort."

"Special group?" Nick asked.

"The VIP Circle, they call it. It's just some silly childish excuse to exclude other club members. A disgrace, I call it."

"Judge Pettigrew," Eileen said, dropping all pretenses, "Chief Wallace told us that certain things have been bothering you about the club. Could you tell us about those things?"

"Well, part of it has to do with that idiotic VIP Circle. This past year it's as if some of the young members have taken over. Old fogies like me— well, we've practically stopped going at all because we've been made to feel so unwelcome. Maybe that's as it should be, but it's a big pill to swallow for those of us who actually helped begin the club."

The judge spread garlic butter on a crusty piece of Italian bread before continuing. "And it's no secret that the club has had operational problems lately. There's been a lawsuit. It was handled out of court, very quietly, thanks to one of the members who's a lawyer. But that's just the tip of the iceberg, I'm afraid. There are staff problems too. Help simply won't stay. There's been a huge turnover of waiters, caddies, and the cleaning staff. I know it's hard to keep good employees these days, but there seems to be a disproportionate number of firings at the club."

"Do you think that—" Nick's question was interrupted by the arrival of another waiter.

"Telephone, Judge Pettigrew."

The judge excused himself and followed the waiter to a phone.

Nick picked up his wineglass and looked around for a thirsty plant. A likely candidate was only a few feet away.

"Don't you dare pour that wine in there," Eileen hissed. She put a hand over her mouth to hide her grin. "It'll kill the plant! Besides, do you have any idea how expensive that wine is?"

Nick set his full glass back on the table.

"Here," Eileen said, "pour some of it into my glass, and it'll look like you've had a few sips. You don't drink?"

"An occasional off-duty beer." He stressed the words *off duty*.

"Eeew. You've got that same self-righteous look my fiancé gets when he preaches at me about drinking too much caffeine."

"You have a fiancé?" Nick asked, dumping half of his untouched wine into Eileen's glass.

"Buddy and I have been engaged two years."

"Two years? Are you trying for the *Guinness Book* world record for long engagements?"

Eileen took a sip of wine and dabbed her lips gently with the napkin. "No—we were supposed to get married three months ago, but we hit a snag. My father's heart condition prevented him from making the trip out here, so we postponed the ceremony. It's really important to me to have my dad at my wedding. He's the only family I've got."

"Where is your dad?"

"Florida. I've been after him to move out here for over a year, but he won't budge. Mom is buried in Jacksonville, and he refuses to leave her."

At that moment the judge returned to the table. "I'm afraid I'm going to have to leave. Pressing business. But please, the dinner tab has already been taken care of. If you're unfamiliar with the specialties of the house, trust Lorenzo," the judge instructed, giving Nick a meaningful look. "He'll never steer you wrong. Or be adventurous. Order whatever you want. Enjoy yourselves."

"I'll walk you out," Nick offered, rising from his seat.

"Nonsense. You stay here with your pretty young lady."

He sees right through me, Nick realized. *He doesn't think I can pass myself off as a scion of society.* "But sir, about the club—"

He patted Nick's shoulder. "Not to worry. Everything has been taken care of. You young folks go on out there Sunday and make yourselves at home. I'll have your membership papers signed, sealed, and delivered by then." The judge leaned closer to the table and lowered his voice. "I trust you will be discreet enough in your investigations to protect the innocent parties at the club. There

160

are a lot of good people there that I wouldn't want to see hurt. And mind you, I'm not saying anything unlawful is going on there at all, but if Ernest Wallace and Bob Henderson think there is, that's good enough for me. I've known both men for years, and they're usually right about these things. What is it you call it, a policeman's hunch?"

"I call it women's intuition," Eileen said, finishing off her wine.

Both men laughed.

"Enjoy yourselves," the judge reminded them before leaving.

Nick scanned a menu, but his mind was elsewhere. "How does your fiancé, Buddy, feel about your being a cop?" he asked.

Eileen lifted her rust-colored eyebrows. "He's fine with it."

"Doesn't he worry about you being in danger?"

"No more than I do about him. Buddy's a fireman."

As Eileen related a story about Buddy hacking his way out of a burning building Nick considered the job for himself. *Maybe I could become a fireman after I quit the police force. I'd still be serving the public, and the job would still be different and challenging.*

No, if I were a fireman, Jessica would only want to be in the middle of that too. He closed his eyes and imagined her climbing a ladder to a ten-story fire, swinging an ax and shouting, "Isn't this fun, Nick? Isn't this the most exciting adventure we've ever shared?"

"You seem preoccupied, Nick. Is anything wrong?"

"No, not really," Nick lied. "I'm just having trouble making up my mind on what to order."

The truth was, he was missing Jessica terribly. He wondered how long she was going to stay mad at him about having Eileen as a partner. *Probably till this case is over*, he thought. *I'm glad she can't see us now. Having wine and—*

Lorenzo, the waiter, appeared and began describing a few of Tucci's most famous original dishes, but Nick didn't hear a word of it. His gaze was frozen to a spot not three feet away. Through the tangle of ferns, trees, and flowers, he could see a furious face pressed against the window.

No, it can't be, he told himself.

But it was.

"Jessica!" he blurted.

"There you are, you low-down, dirty, two-timing, wrong-partner-picking slug!" Jessica snarled as she stared at Nick's surprised face through the steamy window of Tucci's. "You just thought I wasn't smart enough to be a cop, Nick Fox. Well, I tracked you down, didn't I?"

Although her view was slightly blocked by

plants, Jessica could see more than she wanted to see—her boyfriend having dinner with that . . . that *redhead!* "Some serious police work they're doing! All alone, just the two of them. Dressed up like they're on their way to the Oscars. And they're having wine! I thought Nick *hated* wine!"

"Uh-oh. Here he comes," she said as he dashed away from the table. *Probably coming after me,* she thought. *Well, come on! I'm ready to have this out here and now!* As she began backing out of the elaborately landscaped flower bed something grabbed her. She gasped and spun around, only to find the sleeve of Elizabeth's black cashmere sweater caught on a prickly shrub. *Oh no! Liz is gonna kill me. But I had to borrow this sweater. Every piece of clothing I owned that was suitable for police surveillance was dirty.*

She'd hardly freed the snag before she was caught again. *Stupid bush!* she thought. *Why would a restaurant plant bushes that are practically lethal weapons?* She squeezed past yet another dangerous shrub and headed around the side of the restaurant to intercept Nick.

Earlier that evening Jessica had tailed him from his apartment to the Bayside Motel, where he'd picked up Ms. Supercop for their little rendezvous. Then she'd followed them to a small house in the valley where they'd switched from Nick's Camaro to a white Thunderbird. It must have been Bill Fagan's house. She'd heard Nick talk about that car often enough—especially since she'd ruined its stupid hubcap during the chop shop bust. She'd actually saved everyone's lives by flinging that ridiculous metal Frisbee at the ugly guy with the gun—and yet Bill and Nick still expected her to pay for replacing it!

"Some people are never appreciative when you do good things for them," Jessica muttered as she rounded a corner.

Jessica's tailing adventure had nearly ended when she'd lost Nick on the freeway. But when she turned on the Elm exit, thinking she'd just go back to Bill's and wait for Nick to return the Thunderbird, she'd seen the white car in Tucci's parking lot.

If Nick thinks he's doing a good job sneaking around being all incognito and stuff, he'd better learn something about driving such an obvious car, she noted mentally.

She skidded around the side of the building and headed for the restaurant entrance, grumbling all the way. "How *dare* Nick! It's bad enough that he scorns me by having another woman as a partner, but then—to top it all off—he actually takes her out on a date! To dinner in one of the most expensive places in town, no less! Does he take me, the woman he supposedly loves, to dinner at Tucci's? Uh-uh. Takeout Chinese in little cardboard boxes and a rented kick-boxing video—that's a good enough date for dull, boring Jessica. But not for the lady cop."

What's her name again? she wondered. *Irene? Lurleen? Billie Jean? Oh, who cares?*

As she charged into the restaurant Nick grabbed her by the arm and pulled her into the dim little hallway that led to the phones and the rest rooms.

He'd better not try to tell me he's working, she thought. *Not when I've caught him red-handed with my own two eyes.*

"Jessica! What are you doing here!" Nick hissed.

"What am I doing here! You've got a lot of nerve asking me that. What are you doing here . . . with *her?*"

"We *have* to be here, Jessica."

She paused. He looked so devastatingly handsome in his blue blazer that she was momentarily distracted, but then she remembered her mission and shook loose from his grip. "Don't lie to me, Nick. On top of everything else please don't lie."

"This is work."

She rolled her eyes. "Oh, *right,* you both look like you're working *really* hard. Especially Ms. Policewoman in her slinky green number. How stupid do you think I am?"

"We're undercover."

"Sure, you are. Let me guess. You're here at the restaurant, investigating whether Tucci's imported wine is really made by toothless hags

165

stomping grapes in the basement. I can't believe you'd stand here and lie to me, Nick!"

"Why would I lie? You met Eileen yesterday at the station."

"Yeah, I met her all right."

"Jessica, listen to me. This is my *job*. Why would I want to be with someone else when I'm in love with you?"

"That's easy. Because you don't love me. You couldn't love me and treat me this way. You have no respect for how I feel or what I think. It was bad enough when you thought I was too silly and immature to share your work. But now . . . now you think I'm too dull to even share your *life!*"

"Jessica, if you'll just calm down, I'll try to explain to you. . . ."

But Jessica was way beyond listening to his ridiculous excuses. Her heart was breaking into a million pieces. Jessica had been let down by men before, but this time was different. This time she'd been certain that Nick was the one. The one who'd never hurt her. The one who really, truly loved her. Once again she was wrong.

"You are a liar, Nick Fox," she lashed out again. "A cheating, two-timing liar who won't even give his girlfriend a chance." Bursting into angry tears, she ran past the gawking patrons waiting in Tucci's lobby and out into the street.

Chapter Eight

"How's that?" Bruce said as he idly rubbed suntan lotion onto Lila's perfectly tanned, smooth back. Normally the very act of touching her would have contented him, but it was the third time he'd greased her down this morning, and he was beginning to get tired of it.

It was Saturday—the third day in a row that he and Lila had squandered at Verona Springs. "Li, don't you think we're spending way too much time here?" he asked, capping the bottle of coconut oil and wiping his hands on a towel.

"At the pool?" Lila reached for her lemonade and took a long, cooling sip. "I guess we could go inside and sit in the lounge awhile if you'd rather."

"Actually I meant we're spending too much time at the *club*."

"There's no such thing as too much time at the

club. I love it here. I thought you did too. This was your idea, after all."

"I know, but . . . I mean, it's nice to come out here and relax—every once in a while."

"I thought that's what we were doing."

"Lila, we've been out here all day for the past three days!"

"So?"

"So I didn't plan on spending every waking moment of the rest of my life here. Why don't we do something else? Let's go to campus. You haven't been to Theta house in ages. Don't your sorority sisters miss you?"

"Bruce, if you'd actually rather spend time with silly frat boys than with cultured, refined, educated people, why don't you just say so? Don't use my friends as an excuse."

"OK, I'm saying so. I'd like to go visit Sigma house."

"Don't be ridiculous. The Sigmas and the Thetas have nothing that could possibly compare to any of this."

"But don't you think we're overdoing it a bit? We don't have to spend all our time here."

"We do if we hope to become VIPs. I don't know why I have to keep explaining this to you! If we want to be accepted, we have to show our total commitment to the club. They expect loyalty. Not just anyone can be in the VIP Circle, you know."

"I know, I know."

"Bruce, I have to become a VIP. I just have to."

"OK, Lila. I'm sure we both will. . . . It's just a matter of *time*."

"I don't *want* it to be a matter of time. I want it, and I want it *now!*" Suddenly the college Lila he knew and loved had morphed before his very eyes into the spoiled high-school Lila he had fought with for years. Bruce could do nothing except stare in amazement.

"I've been through a lot this past year," she continued. "Is it asking too much to expect a little enjoyment out of life? Why can't you understand how important this is to me?"

Bruce sucked in his pride but was saved from apologizing by the arrival of a waiter, a young man in crisp chinos and a blindingly white polo shirt.

"Miss Fowler, telephone call for you."

Lila huffed at the interruption. "If I'd wanted to be bothered with phone calls at the pool, I'd have brought along my cell phone!"

"I'm sorry, Miss Fowler. Normally I wouldn't bother a guest at the pool, but it's your sister. A family emergency, I'm afraid."

"My sister?" Lila opened her mouth to protest but snapped it shut again.

Good trick for an only child, Bruce thought. *I'd bet my grandma's trust fund it's Jessica Wakefield, who just happened to leave out the fact that she's a sorority sister. Jessica probably doesn't even think of it as a lie.*

"You can take the call in the Cabana Bar," the waiter said politely.

Lila tossed down her towel. "Well, it seems to me you could have at least brought a cordless phone out here!" she mumbled as she followed the waiter to the nearby bar area.

Some inconvenience, Bruce thought. *The bar is probably all of twenty steps away. She's beginning to sound just like Pepper Danforth—and look like her too.* He squinted as he looked at the back of Lila's garish pink swimsuit. To the best of his knowledge, Lila had never owned a single scrap of tacky clothing in her life. Now she had sacks full of the stuff.

Bruce picked up the bottle of suntan oil and smeared a little on his own shoulders. Then he rolled over onto his stomach and laid his head atop his crossed arms. *I might as well work on my own tan if I'm going to be here the rest of the day,* he thought, closing his eyes against the glare that was beginning to give him a headache.

Suddenly Bruce felt an icy tap on his shoulder. He looked up into the blazing sunlight. There, hovering above him, stood Bunny Sterling in an orange, sausage-skin-tight minidress.

Bruce scrambled upright, nearly tipping out of his deck chair in the process. "Um . . . hello there. Uh, Bunny? Bunny Sterling, isn't it?"

"I'm surprised you remember my name."

"Of course I do." Sweat began to pop out

across his forehead as he noticed Pepper standing behind Bunny. *This is it,* he told himself. *They're here to lower the boom. Lila is going to* kill *me!*

"How have you been, Bunny?" he managed to say.

"Just fine, thanks." Bunny gave him a big, toothy grin. "As if *you* care."

"Jessica, I'm sure Nick didn't mean a thing by it." Lila held the phone away from her ear and craned her neck in an attempt to keep an eye on Bruce while she stood in the tiny cubbyhole where the phone had been practically hidden away. But she couldn't see a thing—a potted palm blocked her view. She wanted to hurry and get back before he did something stupid. "What? No, Jess. I don't believe Nick thinks you're a bubbleheaded blonde. . . . Of *course* he doesn't. . . . I'm sure he thinks you're a levelheaded young woman, because you are."

Oh, come on, *Jessica,* Lila pleaded silently. *I feel for you, I really do, but I don't have time to listen to your silly problems right now. Pepper will be here any minute.*

"Jessica," she said with as much sympathy in her tone as she could muster, "I know you'll work things out with Nick. You always do. But you really shouldn't call me here at the club, saying it's an emergency. That gives a very bad impression. . . . No, Jess. I don't think Nick's having a new partner is an emergency." Lila winced at the sound of a receiver being slammed in her ear. She stared at the phone a moment as if it was somehow defective. How dare Jessica hang up on her!

"That Jess, always emotional," Lila said lightly. "She'll be OK. She'll solve her man problems. She always does."

Lila shrugged and hung up the phone. Looking back toward the pool, she could hardly believe her eyes. Bruce was talking to Pepper Danforth and Bunny Sterling!

With a nervous gulp Lila straightened her wide-brimmed straw hat, slipped her sunglasses back onto her nose, and tugged at the bottom of her bright pink swimsuit to make sure it fit just right. It was a Lola Valesquela original—Pepper's favorite designer. She was sure to be impressed.

After a quick, satisfying peek at herself in the mirror over the bar, she hurried toward her friends, but just as she lifted her hand in greeting and opened her mouth to speak, Bruce's voice brought her up short. *What is he doing?* she wondered. *Apologizing? Didn't I tell him to forget about the little fiasco he had with Bunny? Didn't I tell him I'd handle it if he'd just keep his big mouth shut?*

". . . really, Bunny, you know how fraternity parties can be," Bruce was saying. "I hardly knew what I was doing that night. I hope you don't think I left you there all alone on purpose. I guess

I was just going through my wild frat-boy phase. I didn't want to be tied down to a girl, no matter how pretty and talented and well connected she was."

"Don't give it another moment's thought, Bruce. My poor broken heart mended awfully quickly, and besides, if you hadn't dumped me, I never would have been free to meet Paul, my fiancé." She flashed an ostentatiously huge diamond engagement ring in Bruce's face. "Maybe you've heard of him. Paul Krandall? His father is Gregory Krandall, the congressman? I met Paul at a political fund-raiser. My daddy is a big contributor to Krandall's campaign."

"Bunny's father is a famous movie producer, you know," Pepper added.

Lila was mesmerized by the sunlight flashing off Bunny's diamond. It shimmered as Bunny gestured grandly each time she spoke. The ring was so large, it bordered on tasteless, tacky, and gauche.

I've got to get a ring like that, Lila thought, clearing her throat.

"Oh, hello there," Bunny said, glancing coolly in Lila's direction and then back to Bruce. "Aren't you going to introduce me to your lovely girl-friend?"

Lila stepped forward and held out her hand to Bunny. Bunny limply grasped the ends of her fingers for a second, then she looked at her own as if to see if anything had rubbed off on them.

"The reason we wandered over," Pepper began, "was to make sure the two of you were planning to participate in the annual charity tennis tournament next week. Mixed doubles."

"It's a very big affair here at the club," Bunny added, fondling the diamond tennis bracelet at her wrist.

"All the slots are filling up fast. You'd better get your reservations if you haven't already," Pepper said. She dabbed at the corners of her lips, as if to make sure all the smiling she was doing hadn't smeared her lipstick. "Bunny and Paul are playing, aren't you, Bunny?"

"We wouldn't miss it for anything. Paul is so competitive. I'm not, but it's for a good cause, and there'll be scads of celebrities here—thanks to Daddy. He personally knows all the biggest."

"So, are you in?" Pepper asked.

Bruce gulped audibly. "Well—"

"Of course we're in," Lila interrupted, flashing him a quick, wilting glance. "Bruce and I both *adore* tennis, and we would never miss helping out an important cause."

"I thought not," Pepper said. "Oh! I almost forgot. Afterward we're having a little private gathering in the VIP lounge on the third floor. Why don't you two join us—as my guests?"

Lila's heart began to pound. "We'd *love* to."

"Ciao," Pepper said with a wave.

"Ta ta," Bunny called over her shoulder.

Lila watched Pepper and Bunny until they were out of sight before sinking back down onto her chaise longue. She reached over and grabbed Bruce's strong hand. "Bruce," she said with a sigh, looking into his deep blue eyes and smiling. "I think we've done it." She let out a long, loud breath of relief. "We're on our way to becoming bright lights in the Verona Springs social scene!"

"The brightest," he agreed, kissing her hand gently.

While most of the SVU students were hurrying to the cafeteria to get the dreaded Saturday dinner over with, Elizabeth and Nina huddled in the library's research room.

In the quiet, practically deserted room Elizabeth thumbed through recent copies of the *Sweet Valley Gazette* and the *Chronicle* while Nina viewed the older newspaper issues, which were stored on microfiche.

"Thanks for helping me with this," Elizabeth remarked as she reached for her pen to take notes.

"You know me. I'm a sucker for the library," Nina replied with a laugh. "The one night this week I haven't had to be in the library to study, and I come here with you for fun."

"You're a wild and crazy girl, Nina Harper."

"And you're an obsessive newspaper reporter,

Elizabeth Wakefield. I thought you said this story is no big deal."

"It's not . . . probably." She looked up from her notebook sheepishly. "This story may turn out to be just a puff piece, but it never hurts to be informed."

"What exactly am I looking for again?" Nina asked, squinting into the viewer.

"Just copy anything having to do with the Verona Springs Country Club. I don't even know myself what we're looking for, but I'll know it when I see it."

"Spoken like a true journalist," Nina quipped. She was the scientific type, the type who liked to know where she was going before she got there. "So how's it going so far at the newspaper? Over the new-job jitters yet?"

"I love it. I know I was nervous at first, but the minute I walked in the door, I felt at home. It's hard to explain."

"But aren't you going to miss the station and—"

"And?" Elizabeth asked. She lifted an eyebrow meaningfully, but she didn't let Nina answer. "No, I don't think I'm going to miss the station *or* Tom Watts. It's better if he stays out of my sight until my wounds heal."

"Maybe you're right." Nina stretched and rubbed her eyes. "Any cute guys at the paper?"

"Nina!"

"No harm in keeping your eyes open."

"I am definitely not interested. I'm there to work—not scope out new guys. Besides," she said with a giggle. "I haven't seen anyone gorgeous enough to bother with yet."

"What about Scott? I think he's really good-looking."

"Scott's cute, I guess, but . . ."

"But what? Has he asked you out?"

"No. But . . . well, it's a long story. He's starting to make me nervous. It seems like everywhere I go, he's there."

"Oh, big surprise. And exactly where have you been lately?"

Elizabeth grinned. "The newspaper office . . . OK, I get your drift. Of *course* he'd be at the newspaper office, but it's not just that. It's like he's always right in my face . . . touching me."

"If it bothers you, tell him to back off."

"I don't think he means anything by it." Elizabeth folded one paper neatly and picked up another one. "He's just one of those touchy-feely people. You know the type. They stand practically on your toes and have to pat your hand while they talk or hug you to say hello and good-bye."

"Are you sure he's touchy-feely with every-body?"

"What do you mean?"

"Maybe he just likes touching *you*." Nina pointed at Elizabeth and widened her dark brown eyes. "Maybe he's interested and doesn't know how to tell you."

"I don't think so. Besides, even if he were, it wouldn't do him any good. I'm not available. I have enough troubles just sorting through my feelings about Todd and Tom. I need another guy like I need another midterm."

"Tell me about it!" Nina returned to the viewer. "Hey, I found the magic words, Verona Springs." She adjusted the focus. "You want a description of Bunny Sterling's deb gown? Or how about a blow-by-blow account of Pepper Danforth winning the charity golf tourney two years ago?"

"Yeah, sure. Make a copy of both. It sounds like exciting reading," Elizabeth drawled sarcastically. But her words died out as her eyes caught on an item in the paper she was holding. "Wow, look. This is interesting."

A shadow fell across the newspaper almost before she got the words out of her mouth. "That was quick!" she remarked, turning around and expecting to see Nina reading over her shoulder. Instead she found the crystal blue eyes of Scott Sinclair.

"Hi." He grinned casually. "I thought I'd find you here. You are one dedicated lady, you know that? Most people would just head over to the country club, write up a few descriptions, and let it go at that."

"I'm not most people."

"You sure aren't." Scott leaned closer and looked at the paper. "I heard you say something was interesting. What'd you find?"

"This." Elizabeth tapped the paper. Nina squeezed conspicuously between her and Scott and peered over Elizabeth's shoulder. "It's nothing but a tiny little blurb," Elizabeth continued, "but it says the body of a murder victim was found in the Verona Springs Reservoir last week."

"How unreal," Nina complained. "Some society lady named after a kitchen spice gets a half-page spread describing her golf attire, and a murder report gets an inch of coverage. What gives?"

"The club probably covered it up to avoid the bad publicity," Scott explained. "They have their reputation to protect, you know."

"But they don't own the newspapers, do they?" Nina asked rhetorically. "What else does it say, Liz?"

"Just the name of the victim, Dwayne Mendoza, and that he was an SVU student working part-time as a caddy."

"He was a student here?"

"That's what it says. Have either of you ever heard the name?"

Scott shook his head. "We never heard anything about this at the paper."

"I haven't either," Nina said. "Maybe it was on the campus news or something."

"I wouldn't know," Elizabeth said pointedly. "I haven't watched the campus news in a while."

Neither Nina nor Scott seemed to catch her sarcasm.

Nina elbowed her way closer to the paper. "Does it say how he was killed or who they think did it or—"

Elizabeth shook her head. "Nothing else. That's it. But I think this might be what I was looking for. There's obviously more to the Verona Springs Country Club than meets the eye."

"I can't believe it. A student from right here at the university was murdered, and we didn't even hear about it," Nina mumbled.

"Here, let me make a copy of that for you," Scott suggested. His body brushed against Elizabeth's back, and his hand touched hers as he reached for the paper.

Elizabeth felt her whole body stiffen at his touch. *It's nothing,* she told herself. *It was just an accident.*

Saturday night and here I sit in this stupid dorm room . . . alone! Jessica slammed her Western civ book shut and gave up even the pretense of studying. *How can this be happening to me, of all people? I must be the only person left in the whole dorm. Probably the only person on the whole* campus *without something fun to do.*

She felt abandoned. Lila was too totally absorbed

by her precious country club to even talk with her on the phone. Isabella was out with Danny. Most of Jessica's other Theta sisters had gone to a party at Zeta house, which Jessica could have attended if she was in any mood to party—which she wasn't. But even if she had been, she couldn't go to a party without Nick. Most depressing of all, even *Elizabeth* was out somewhere.

As the phone started to ring, Jessica threw herself onto her bed and pulled a purple pillow over her head. It had to be Nick. He'd called about umpteen times today, and she was getting tired of it.

" . . . eight . . . nine . . . ten . . . eleven!" she shouted aloud. That time Nick had let the phone ring eleven times. When would he take the hint and realize she wasn't going to answer? Ever! She *never* wanted to talk to him again. She'd even turned off the answering machine so she didn't have to hear his voice.

He acted like she was being unreasonable, like she didn't have any reason to be mad at him. But she did. Every time she closed her eyes, she could see Nick laughing it up with that redhead in that fancy restaurant.

He probably went right back into the restaurant after I left last night and finished his date. He probably laughed about his silly jealous girlfriend all the way through dessert. For all I know, he probably went home with her. Maybe their serious police work lasted all night! I'll bet he didn't give me another thought until this morning, when he got to the station and saw my picture on his desk.

Jessica groaned. Thinking of the station brought a new scenario to mind. She could just imagine Nick sitting around with the other detectives, telling them about how she'd followed him to the restaurant and made a fool of herself. She could just hear him laughing about how silly she was to think for a minute that she could ever be his partner.

Tears threatened to fall, but Jessica grabbed a tissue and wiped them away. *I'm not going to cry,* she told herself. *I'm too mad to cry.*

When the phone started ringing again, Jessica threw a shoe at it, sending it to the floor with a final ding and a clang. She left it lying there until it began wailing with that obnoxious siren noise that the phone company apparently thought was a clever way of informing customers that their phone was off the hook.

"OK, I hear you!" she shouted at the phone before returning the receiver to its cradle and slamming the phone back onto her desk. Suddenly Jessica remembered there was only one place in Dickenson Hall to escape phone bells—the shower.

Jessica grabbed her fuzzy purple robe and began the search for her shower things. *Hmmm . . . first things first. Now where is my shampoo?* She rummaged through the assortment of beauty products strewn across the top of her desk, finding no shampoo but overturning a bottle of perfume that Nick had given her. She tossed it into the wastebasket. *There. That's what I think of your presents, Nick Fox.*

She pulled open her bottom desk drawer. Elizabeth kept file folders in hers, but Jessica was more practical. It was a good, deep drawer, just right for tall bottles of shampoo, lotion, hair spray, and other essentials. But the shampoo wasn't there either.

Then she noticed that the handle of the little plastic bucket she kept her soap and razor in was sticking out from under the edge of her bed. She got down on her hands and knees and reached for it. But along with the bucket she accidentally dragged out a teddy bear that Nick had won for her at the fair. It had practically been their first date, way before she'd even known he was a cop.

She wrapped her fingers around the bear's throat and shook it. *"You,"* she shouted at the bear. "I don't want you around here anymore!" She tossed it over to Elizabeth's clean bed. "Enjoy your new home in Elizabethland."

She still had no shampoo. "Oh, I remember." She jumped up and ran to her closet. There it was, under a pile of towels. Right where she'd thrown it after this morning's shower. As she dug it out she ran across a T-shirt that Nick had bought her at the Bobby Hornet concert. "Ugh! This whole room is booby-trapped with Nick memorabilia," she said with a groan.

Suddenly, in a whirl of fury, she began to gather up everything in her room that reminded her of Nick Fox. The dried crumbly corsage that she'd worn when they went to a sweetheart dinner at Theta house . . . some seashells they'd found on the beach . . . a napkin from that ritzy French restaurant, Andre's.

"It's over, Nick Fox," Jessica said aloud. "If you can't treat me with a little basic respect, then I don't want anything to do with you *or* your junk!" She spied a cardboard box on Elizabeth's desk. *That's just what I need.* She dumped the papers and folders from the box onto Elizabeth's desk and started throwing all her keepsakes and mementos into the box.

A strip of pictures taken at the mall in one of those photo machines . . . a pair of Nick's sunglasses . . . a dried-up rose . . . a love note . . .

"Hey, Jess." Elizabeth stepped into the room and methodically slipped her keys over the hook beside the door. "What're you doing home on a Sat—oh, my gosh!" She grabbed the back of a chair with one hand and clutched her throat dramatically with the other. "What's going on? You aren't cleaning the room, are you?"

"Don't get your hopes up." Jessica figured her twin was about to nag at her for taking her precious cardboard box, but she didn't give her a chance. "For your information, I'm gathering up everything in this room that reminds me of Detective Nick Fox, and I'm going to take it to the police station tomorrow and dump it over his lying head. I'm going to tell him he can keep his memories, 'cause that's all he'll get from me—for the rest of his miserable cheating life!"

Chapter
Nine

"Wow, Toto, I don't think we're in Kansas anymore," Elizabeth said Sunday morning as she drove through the filigreed wrought iron gates of the Verona Springs Country Club. Ahead of them the sprawling pastel yellow clubhouse with its red tiled roof lay nestled in every imaginable shade of green. Across the lawns on their left, automatic sprinklers spewed out rainbows in the midmorning sun. On their right flowers of every imaginable color bloomed in well-defined rows.

Scott whistled appreciatively. "And this must be Emerald City. What have you come to ask the wizard for, little girl?"

"A story," Elizabeth replied quickly.

Scott seemed disappointed with her answer, but she didn't care. She knew what she was here for, and she wasn't going to be swayed by the grandeur of the place.

As they moved along the long, palm-lined driveway Elizabeth slowed the Jeep to a crawl so she could better admire the scene unfolding before her eyes. "What a view! Look at that marble fountain."

"I never knew a place like this existed around here," Scott said.

"I don't think we were meant to. This is a secret fantasy world for a privileged few."

"And yet here we are."

"Yes, here we are. Did you bring your camera?"

"Got it right here." Scott picked his camera up off the floor of the Jeep and showed it to her.

"Why don't you get a shot of the clubhouse from here," Elizabeth suggested, stopping the Jeep long enough for Scott to take a couple of pictures.

"Want me to get a shot of the gates and the guardhouse?" he asked, twisting around in his seat.

"Good idea. I know we brought the camera for taking pictures of Pepper and her friends, but get a lot of shots of the scenery and get candids of the guests too—if you can take them without being noticed. I know we won't be able to use them without permission, but they may come in handy as memory joggers later."

"Do you think the direct approach will work with this Danforth person?"

"From the impression I got on the phone, Pepper Danforth is about as direct as a freeway detour. No, I think the subtle approach will work best. Let her do most of the talking."

"What about the murder?"

"Don't mention anything about the murder unless she brings it up. Let's keep it light and friendly, at least for today." Elizabeth pulled the Jeep into the parking lot and unsnapped her seat belt. "Anyway, I'm not even sure that's the story we're after. The club members may have nothing to do with the murder. They might not have even heard about it. For all we know, the guy was murdered somewhere else and brought here. Just keep your eyes and ears open, and we'll go with whatever we feel."

"I don't know what to talk about with these rich snobs."

"Just talk about the upcoming tennis tournament. Everyone keeps mentioning that it's a charity tournament, but have you noticed that no one has bothered to say what specific charity the proceeds are going to? Ask what other good works they do. Give them compliments—I know you're good at that," she assured him with a smile.

"But it's easy complimenting you. And I hope you don't think it's empty flattery. I've meant every word I've said."

Elizabeth turned her head away to keep Scott from seeing her blush. It seemed as if he could turn anything into an excuse to compliment her. She slipped the strap of her purse over her shoulder and waited for the warm flush of embarrassment to leave her face. "Well, just say whatever feels natural. I don't have a script for the day. Just try to keep Pepper and her friends satisfied for now. It's not like we're here to impress anyone. They know we're reporters, so just be yourself." She reached for the door handle, but Scott stopped her by reaching across the seat and laying his hand on her leg.

"Don't forget, we have to pose as a couple," he said softly.

"I won't forget." She lifted his hand from her leg and placed it back in his own lap. "But don't get carried away, OK? I don't think these are the kind of people who are impressed by public displays of affection, if you know what I mean."

Neither Nick's dress shoes nor Eileen's heels made a sound on the thick Oriental carpet as they crossed through the main lobby of the clubhouse.

"Can you believe the judge's grandson?" Nick said. "I practically burst out laughing the first time he spoke."

"Anderson? He seemed OK to me. What was so funny?"

"His accent. He sounded just like Thurston Howell the Third."

Eileen didn't crack a smile.

"Don't tell me you've never seen *Gilligan's Island*." *Jessica would have gotten it*, Nick thought. *Not only would she have thought it hilarious, she'd have probably gone into her impression of Ginger, the slinky movie star.*

"Nick, I'm sure I watched the same old reruns of *Gilligan's Island* that you did when I was growing up. I just don't see the humor. Different people have different ways of speaking. That doesn't mean we should necessarily make fun of them."

He blinked in amazement at her sudden reprimand. Evidently her day hadn't gone any better than his. "You're right," he apologized. "Sorry." He opened the front door for her, and they started down the long, canopy-covered walkway to the parking lot.

"I'll tell you whose speech was funny, though," she said, surprising him with a sneaky grin.

"Whose?"

"Yours. I can't believe you actually said, 'How do you do?' when Anderson and Pepper introduced themselves."

"Hey, I couldn't let them think I was a commoner."

"And I think next visit we can dress a little more casually."

"I agree with you there. How were we supposed to know that Armani suits wouldn't be the Sunday afternoon attire of choice?"

She tucked a strand of auburn hair behind her

191

ear and regarded him with cool, golden eyes. All traces of her grin had disappeared. "We should have checked things out better."

"I know," he admitted softly. *As if I haven't told myself that about a million times today,* Nick thought dismally. He'd been scolding himself all morning for his obvious lack of preparation. He'd been naive to think that he'd automatically fit right in at the club just because Judge Pettigrew said so. Evidently the judge was a little out of touch with what was acceptable here at the new and improved Verona Club. Nick hadn't been able to put his finger on his exact error yet, but something had been wrong. His look? His attitude? Whatever it was had kept him so successfully ignored, he had felt like the Invisible Man.

"All in all, I'd say our debut appearance fell a little short of the mark, wouldn't you?" she asked.

"I'd say so, my de-ah," Nick said in his best Thurston Howell the Third imitation, hoping to tease the stern look off her face. "I didn't get a nibble about the VIP Circle, did you?"

"Nope. Evidently you have to go through channels. But while you were getting your behind beat by the club's tennis pro, I met a guy named Roger Pierpont, and he did mention the Couples-Only group. He said he thought I'd fit right in. Said we should talk to Pepper Danforth."

"Good. We're on the right track, then."

Eileen paused and looked around to see if they

could be overheard. "Did anyone mention the murder?" she asked.

"Not a word. You'd think it might be on people's minds—even if just for the curiosity factor. A dead body found on the property has to be out of the ordinary."

"Most places," Eileen said cryptically. "So, what next?"

"I don't know. I think I'll come back tomorrow and try to maneuver my way into Anderson's golf foursome. Even if I'm ignored, I'll have a chance to get a peek at the crime scene and talk with the other caddies. I think you should meet me here later for supper in the main dining room. Maybe by then I'll have convinced Anderson and Pepper to join us."

"What about this upcoming tennis tournament? It seems to be a pretty big deal around here. Do you think we should sign up?"

"Do you play tennis?" Nick asked.

She crinkled her freckled nose. "I played quite badly in high school, but I think with a little practice, I'd do better than you did today."

"OK, so I'm a little rusty," he admitted with a grin. "Some job we've got, huh? Faking sports, hanging out in a joint like this?"

"I know," Eileen agreed. "Everything about this place is unbelievable. I've learned more about conspicuous consumption today than I did in two semesters of econ."

"Tell me about it. Just look at this parking lot." Nick tried to keep the envy out of his voice. "A black Testarossa, a red Lamborghini, a silver Porsche, a black Porsche, a wicked yellow Corvette—"

"Oh, it's not that bad," Eileen interrupted. "There's a gray Toyota—just like mine, I might add—and a plain old red Jeep."

"A what?" When Nick spun around, he saw a red Jeep parked on the other side of the parking lot. It looked just like the one Jessica shared with Elizabeth. *Just one more thing to remind me of Jessica,* Nick thought. Then he looked more closely. It wasn't a Jeep *like* the Wakefields'; it *was* the Wakefields'. He recognized the dent Jessica had put in the left front fender. He gasped as a slender blond woman came out from behind the Jeep. Surely Jessica hadn't followed him out here too! As badly as he wanted to see her, he couldn't face another scene like the one at Tucci's.

No, it isn't Jess, he realized. *It's Elizabeth.*

Nick quickly ducked behind Bill Fagan's white Thunderbird, dragging Eileen with him.

"What is it?" Eileen asked, her hand moving automatically to the shoulder holster she wore under her blazer.

"It's my girlfriend's twin sister."

Eileen relaxed her stance and let out an exasperated sigh.

"Our cover could be blown if we run into people we know," Nick remarked, his mind reeling.

Eileen nodded. "You're right." Hunkering down next to Nick, she peeked over the top of the car's hood. "Oh, wow. They're totally identical!"

"You've seen Jessica?"

"I briefly met her at the station, remember? And I also caught her little performance at the restaurant Friday night."

Nick groaned. "I was hoping I'd spared you that pleasure."

"She's quite the spitfire, isn't she?"

Nick smiled. "That's one way to describe her, I guess. I like to say that Jessica just has a lot of energy."

"I take it she's the jealous type. She doesn't trust you to work with me."

"I think she trusts me; it's just—"

"She doesn't trust me? It's OK, Nick, I've run into this problem before. Cop wives are notoriously jealous of female police officers. Would you like for me to call her? I could explain to her that I'm engaged and that you and I are strictly business."

"No, I don't think that'd help. It's not that she's the jealous type. . . . Well, she *can* be, but I don't think that's what's really bothering her. See, she has this crazy idea in her head that if I need a partner to work undercover, it should be her. I think she's seen too many cop shows and thinks it'd be fun."

"Hmmm. *That's* a different version of the jealousy story."

Nick chuckled. "That's a good word for Jessica—different."

Elizabeth and some guy passed only two cars over from where Nick and Eileen crouched. *Whew! That was close,* he thought. *Thank goodness Elizabeth didn't see us.* Nick wasn't as worried about blowing his cover as he was about word getting back to Jessica that Elizabeth had seen him at the club with Eileen. Jessica was already mad enough. Why throw lighter fluid onto an already smoldering fire?

Suddenly his own problems cleared a moment, and his brain returned to logical processing. What in the world was Elizabeth Wakefield doing at the Verona Springs Country Club?

Tom couldn't help but smile at Dana's exuberance as they walked toward the Great Lawn of the country club. She looked like a fairy sprite dancing across the grass, even if she was the weirdest-dressed fairy sprite he'd ever seen.

He was certain she must have bought her high-waisted purple smock dress off the little girls' rack. It was so short, her red bicycle shorts peeked out from underneath. But maybe that was intentional since they matched the cherry red high-top tennis shoes and the giant plastic seventies-style bracelets she was wearing. She was a delight to be around, but he doubted her offbeat sense of style would be appreciated as much at the Verona Springs

Country Club as it was in the music building on campus. This place was so stuffy, he was almost surprised someone hadn't stopped them at the gate and handed them an engraved copy of the dress code.

Or maybe they had. When he'd filled out his membership application, he'd been given a packet of club policies fatter than his Greek philosophy textbook, but he hadn't bothered to wade through any of it yet. *Well,* he thought, *we'll just have to wait and see. If they kick us out, they kick us out. It's George's money, not mine.*

"Isn't this place spectacular?" Dana exclaimed. "Look at those flowers—birds of paradise. Isn't that a marvelous name for a flower? I just love them. They're so, so . . ."

"Big," Tom supplied.

"No," she said with a giggle. "I was going to say bright, exotic, something like that. Did you know I took botany one semester? I'll bet you thought I never took any classes except music, didn't you?"

He looked into her upturned face, which was hard to do since she was wearing a purple floppy-brimmed hat with a pom-pom–size red fake flower pinned right to the front. "Dana, you're crazy. Do you know that?"

"Yes. I'm crazy about *you.*" She hugged him and planted a quick kiss on his lips. "And I'm crazy about this place. Can you believe they have a string quartet here every single afternoon?" She danced a few steps ahead and then back to his side. "I wonder if any of the musicians are from the college. I know Anthony plays somewhere on the weekends. If he's here, I want you to meet him. I know you'll like him."

"Anthony?" Tom asked.

She stopped and put one hand up to prevent her large purple hat from being lifted off her head by a sudden breeze. "You know. Anthony Davidovic, my orchestral music professor. I've told you about him lots of times."

"Oh yeah, I remember. He's your cello tutor, right?"

"Right." Her eyes widened, and she cocked her head to one side. "Listen—I can hear them. They're playing the first movement from Vivaldi's *Four Seasons*. 'Spring.' How appropriate. What else would you play out here in a garden?" Dana kept chattering like a magpie. But for once Tom was glad to hear her go off on one of her music tangents; it left him free to think his own thoughts.

I'm going to like it here. If ever there was a place that could make me forget about work and school and—oh, who am I trying to kid? I'm going to think about Elizabeth no matter where I am. But at least I know one thing for sure—this is a place where I definitely won't *have to worry about running into her. Elizabeth would rather be dressed in Jessica's skimpiest bikini and put on display in the quad than come to a place like this.*

" . . . we've practiced Debussy's cello sonata, but I think we'll probably go with the Haydn piece for the spring concert. Anthony prefers Corelli, so we may end up doing that, but I like Haydn better, don't you?" Dana's dark curls bounced around her head as she hurried a few steps ahead of him.

I really do enjoy being with Dana, he thought. *She's cute and friendly and really a lot of fun. Most of all, she keeps my mind off . . . someone else.*

"Are you paying any attention to me, Tom?" Dana asked, coming back and blocking his path.

As he looked down at her, standing there in that goofy hat, he couldn't help it; he laughed right out loud. The sound almost startled him. It felt so good to laugh again. From the strain he was feeling in his facial muscles, he realized he hadn't been smiling nearly enough lately. *Well, today I'm going to laugh and be happy,* he told himself. *This is another world, where I can relax and have a good time. Nothing outside the walls of the Verona Springs Country Club can touch me today.*

"Yes, Dana, I'm paying attention to you." He swooped her up into a big hug that brought her feet completely off the ground. "Only to you."

"Let's sit over there," Dana suggested after he'd placed her back on her feet. But as they threaded their way toward the only vacant table the quartet quit playing.

"Oh, great. Now they're going on break," Dana said disappointedly. "I don't want to just sit here and wait. Let's take a walk until they come back. I hear they have one of those garden mazes here. I've always wanted to try to find my way through one. And I hear they're really romantic. Let's go try it out until the quartet comes back." She tugged playfully on his arm. "Maybe we can find a private spot where I can thank you properly for bringing me to this wonderful place."

With a grin Tom let himself be led away from the Great Lawn toward the garden maze.

These things are always so impressive in the movies, Tom thought, looking at the shady entrance. *I guess that's because they're usually shot from above—a bird's-eye view. Down here on the ground, from a guy's-eye view, it just looks like a seven-foot-tall row of hedges.*

Dana tugged his arm again and giggled. "Come on. What are we waiting for?"

Just as they turned the corner around the first row of tall hedges Tom noticed a couple coming along the narrow path toward them. Their heads were bent close together, and they were whispering confidentially to each other. Suddenly Tom's stomach plummeted as if he'd gone over the first drop of a roller coaster. He stopped and stared. He couldn't believe his eyes. The couple looked just like—

"What is it, Tom? What's wrong?" Dana asked, her grip on his arm tightening.

Tom couldn't answer. He could only stare straight ahead at the advancing couple, who apparently hadn't seen them yet.

"That's Elizabeth, isn't it?" Dana murmured.

Yes, it was. The very last person he'd expected to see at the Verona Springs Country Club had just materialized in front of him.

"Who's that she's with?" Dana continued. "I thought she was dating Todd Wilkins. Do you think that's her new boyfriend?"

Words failed Tom completely as he stared at Elizabeth's beautiful, unsuspecting face. She was with that ex-WSVU intern again. Although Tom had talked himself out of the idea after seeing them Thursday, it appeared that they were, indeed, a couple. As adrenaline pumped into Tom's system he felt like running away, but it was too late. Elizabeth's eager expression had suddenly changed into a wide-eyed look of horror that told him she'd seen him as well.

Tom quickly dropped Dana's arm. But almost at the same instant Scott possessively snatched up Elizabeth's hand. In retaliation Tom put his arm around Dana's shoulders and pulled her close. The movement was so abrupt, she had to grab her hat to keep it from falling off.

The air around Tom crackled as if it were alive with static electricity. And when his eyes met

Elizabeth's, he felt the inevitable shock, just as surely as if he'd stuck his finger in a socket.

Although the path was as smooth and level as a ballroom floor, Elizabeth stumbled over her own two feet. She was surprised that the very sight of Tom Watts could still affect her so. She'd thought she'd flushed him out of her system once and for all after the funeral. So why was her heart beating like a hummingbird's wings?

Scott must have thought she was falling because he'd quickly grabbed her hand for support. She was grateful for his kindness, but for some odd reason she didn't want Tom to see them holding hands. She tugged slightly to free her hand, but Scott's grip only tightened. Well, it didn't matter. Not with the way Tom was hugging Dana.

When Dana slipped her arms possessively around Tom and leaned her head against his shoulder, Elizabeth felt as if she had been stabbed in the heart. She gritted her teeth as pangs of jealousy bubbled up from her churning stomach. *She* should have been the one at Tom's side—not Dana Upshaw.

Why should I care? she thought. *I don't. I don't care.* But no matter how hard she tried to convince herself of that, she knew it wasn't true. She would never love anyone the way she'd loved Tom. As her panic grew, she glanced nervously around. She wanted to run away. She had to! But there was only one way out of the maze that she knew of, and Tom was blocking her path. There was no escape—nothing to do but stand firm. She took a deep breath, looked right into his dark, smoldering eyes, and steeled herself for the scathing remarks she was certain would follow. Ever since the moment she'd told Tom that his father had kissed her, Tom had never passed up an opportunity to say something awful to her.

"So," Tom said after what seemed like an eternity. "I noticed you left WSVU."

Elizabeth opened her mouth, but her vocal cords were paralyzed. She couldn't make a single sound come out. Dumbly she nodded. *Just smile,* she told herself. *Be polite and avoid confrontation. Get through this as quickly as possible and be on your way.*

"She's working at the *Gazette* now," Scott explained. But Tom's gaze never flickered away from Elizabeth's face.

"You just waltz in when no one's around and clear out your desk. That's a pretty cowardly way to leave a job, don't you think?" His chin jutted forward belligerently.

The anger stirred up by his words and haughty, superior tone not only made Elizabeth forget her resolution to be polite, but it apparently gave her back the use of her voice. "Well, I wasn't getting many prime stories assigned to me at the TV station," she exclaimed.

"If you'd showed up once in a while, you might have gotten an assignment or two!" Tom shouted back.

Elizabeth bristled. How dare he!

"The place has been a mess," he continued. "We've been totally swamped lately. As if we weren't already short staffed, we had two new interns quit." Tom stared pointedly at Scott.

Scott stepped forward as if to explain, but she elbowed him aside. This was between her and Tom.

"Are you going to blame me for Scott's quitting too?" she shouted. "You might as well—you blame me for everything else. Why not throw in mud slides, forest fires, earthquakes, ozone depletion?"

"We have so much work to do, and you just walk out." Tom threw up his hands. "For someone who's always been so responsible, it was a pretty low-down thing to do."

A twinge of guilt nagged at her. He seemed genuinely upset by her leaving. Had she really abandoned Tom and the station at a time when they'd needed her?

But Tom didn't stop there. "I think you could have at least told someone, Elizabeth. Don't you think that would have been the mature thing to do? Oh yes, I forgot. Maturity is one of those basic concepts you haven't quite grasped yet."

His contemptuous tone made her blood boil

again. "I did tell someone. I told Professor Sedder. Contrary to what you may believe, *he's* the one officially in charge of the station. Maybe *you* should check in with your boss once in a while."

Tom's face reddened, and his nostrils flared. His mouth opened a few times as if he were a fish out of water.

Ha! Elizabeth thought triumphantly. *Now you know what it's like to not have a ready comeback.* "If you will kindly step out of our way, we have work to do," she said with more dignity than she knew she possessed.

It seemed as if all four of them were about to speak at once, but suddenly the hedges rustled beside them and a gardener appeared. In his drab olive pants and shirt, covered with bits of leaves, sticks, grass clippings, and dirt, he was practically camouflaged. "Pardon me," he said quietly. He dipped his head until they could see only the top of his dirty straw hat. "You must forgive me, but I heard you say work." He snipped a time or two at the hedges with large old-fashioned clippers. "You are here from the college looking for work?"

"We're from the college," Elizabeth began, "but—"

"Go home," he said, not letting her explain. "Go back to school. Work at the burger place. Work at the doughnut shop. Go away from this place."

"No, you don't understand," Scott said.

The gardener glanced up at them from his stooped position. His face, tanned to the appearance of a dark, leathery mask, held a disturbing look. *What is it?* Elizabeth wondered. *Dislike? Distrust? Fear? Is he afraid of us?*

"Please, go." He spoke rapidly with a slight accent. "Go away."

"What's wrong with being from the college?" Scott asked indignantly.

"I like the college," the gardener said. "My nephew, he went to the university. He was a good boy. Very smart. Very hard worker. He paid all his tuition by working here at the club. Dwayne was the first person in our whole family to go to college."

"We're not here to work," Tom explained. "We're members."

Animation seemed to drain from the gardener's face. "Sorry. Forget I said anything," the man mumbled hastily before he scurried away.

"Wait," Elizabeth called. "Wait, sir!"

He paused but didn't look up. "Sorry . . . I cannot talk to members."

"Sir," Elizabeth persisted. Something the old man said had jogged her brain. Suddenly the article she'd read in the paper about the murdered caddy flashed into focus. "Excuse me, sir, you said your nephew's name was Dwayne. Was it Dwayne Mendoza?"

If there had been doubt about the man's

expression before, there was none now. Fear practically sparked from his eyes. "I cannot talk to members. I will lose my job," he said, turning the corner and heading for the center of the maze.

"Wait, don't go. I'm not a member!" Elizabeth hurried after him. She caught his arm. "Was Dwayne Mendoza your nephew?"

He nodded. "I am Juan Mendoza."

"Please, Mr. Mendoza. It's OK. You can trust me. I'm not a member of the club. My name is Elizabeth Wakefield, and I'm a newspaper reporter here to do a story. Won't you talk with me, please?"

Mr. Mendoza seemed unsure, but at least he was no longer trying to run away.

"Your nephew—was he drowned here at the club?"

Mr. Mendoza looked around nervously but nodded again.

"Do you know something more about his death?" Elizabeth asked quietly.

Mr. Mendoza removed his hat and began twisting the brim in his hands. "I heard them talking. I followed them. It was very dark. I was afraid. I couldn't see them, but I heard—"

At that moment Tom, Dana, and Scott appeared around the corner. Mr. Mendoza stuck the hat back on his head and glared at the advancing trio. He turned quickly to Elizabeth. "You go, pretty one. It is not safe here. Some people think they're above the law—that they can get away with murder." With that announcement he dashed around the corner and out of sight.

"Hey, wait!" Tom yelled. "What's this all about? I'm from the campus TV station. . . ."

"I'm from the newspaper," Scott bellowed over Tom's voice as he fumbled with the camera hanging around his neck. "Can you give us a quote?"

"What's going on?" Dana asked petulantly. "I'll bet the quartet is starting again and we're missing it."

Elizabeth ran after Mr. Mendoza, but he had simply vanished into the lush greenery of the maze.

"I knew I'd uncover something about that murder here," Elizabeth said excitedly. "I just knew it!"

Tom started after Elizabeth and the gardener, but he'd hardly taken two steps when he was practically tackled by Dana.

"Tom, what's going on?" she whined.

"I don't know." *But I'd sure like to,* he added mentally as he watched Scott disappear in the direction Elizabeth had gone. He took a step after them, but Dana dug in her red high-tops and tugged him to a stop.

"Forget about them. Let them go."

By the time Tom had untangled himself from

Dana's grasp, he knew it was too late. He couldn't catch up to the old man now, and neither would Elizabeth or Scott. The wily old gardener would never be found in the maze—unless he wanted to be. The way the man was dressed made him practically invisible among the lush foliage to begin with, and even more important, he probably knew the maze inside and out. He could hide forever.

There's a story here, Tom thought. *I saw that familiar "I'm-onto-something" light go on in Elizabeth's eyes. No one can sniff out a story like Liz. She knows something, but what?*

It was somehow connected to that gardener; he knew that much. Maybe he could find the man and ask him to come to the station for an interview. But first he needed to know what was going on. The man had warned them away from jobs. Was he trying to discourage college students from taking jobs so his friends could get employment at the club? Maybe. He was obviously Latino. An illegal alien? No, it didn't ring true.

Something else nagged at Tom. What was it the old man had said just before he'd run off? Something about getting away with murder. Did he mean it figuratively or literally?

Elizabeth and Scott returned without the gardener. Tom couldn't take his eyes off Elizabeth's flushed face. She was slightly out of breath. Yes, there was no doubt about it. Elizabeth was here for a story. It was the only logical explanation for why she'd be here in the first place.

What had happened that he didn't know about? It tore at his insides that Elizabeth knew and he didn't. How he wished the two of them could rush back to their office and brainstorm this whole thing.

Our office? What am I thinking? It's my office. She works for the newspaper now. Scott Sinclair has stolen away my girl— and my best reporter.

"Tom, are we going to stand here wasting the whole afternoon?" Dana griped.

Tom looked at her crossly. Her whining was starting to get to him. Suddenly his own ambition kicked in. *Well, I was writing news before Miss Elizabeth Wakefield ever stepped into my life, and I can still write news without her. I'll find that gardener and I'll show* her *a thing or two about how to dig out a story.*

Despite his adrenaline rush Tom felt conflicted. He didn't want to compete with Elizabeth over this story, and not just because she was one of the best reporters he'd ever known. That sort of competition didn't scare him. But if Elizabeth found out he was after her story, not only would she be hurt, but she'd be furious. It'd ruin any possible hope of reconciliation—not like there seemed to be any at the moment.

Tom watched as Elizabeth leaned close to Scott and whispered something. Tom wanted to slap away Scott's hands, which were constantly touching, caressing her arms, her face. . . .

I guess there's no hope of reconciliation, he realized. If she was going to crush his heart by not responding to his heartfelt apology letter, and by dating who-knew-who else, and by flaunting those dates in front of him, then he'd just have to fight back the only way he had left—professionally. *OK, Elizabeth. This is war. We'll see who's the better journalist.*

Chapter Ten

One case down and about a million more to go, Nick thought as he slapped a fat manila folder shut and shoved it to one side of his crowded desk. He stretched his arms, rotated his stiff shoulder muscles, and yawned. What he wouldn't give for a long, hot shower and a nap. He was still dressed in the same suit he'd worn to the country club that morning, minus the coat and tie. He'd hoped to finish the paperwork on these old cases so he could concentrate on the Verona Springs case, but he'd swear the stack of case files on his desk was growing. It was days like this that made him think it wouldn't be so bad to give up police work after all.

"How's it going, partner?" Eileen asked as she sauntered into the room.

"If one more thing goes wrong today, I think I'll go crazy," he replied.

"You look like you could use a few hours of sleep, Detective."

"Sleep? What's that?"

She poured herself a cup of coffee and took a sip as she walked toward Nick's desk. Her eyes grew wide, and she gulped, but he had to hand it to her—she was one tough lady. She didn't spit it out or even choke. *Someone should have warned her about Dub's coffee,* he thought with a chuckle.

"If you've been drinking this," she began after clearing her throat, "I can see why you haven't slept." She stared at the noxious black liquid in her cup.

Nick held up an empty coffee cup. "Dub beat us to the coffeemaker today. If his spoon won't stand up straight in the cup, he thinks it's for wimps."

"You've been here since we got back from the club?"

"'Fraid so."

"Did you ever get through to your girlfriend?"

Nick's heart suddenly felt as dark as Dub's coffee. "No. I've called all day. She's still not answering the phone—not for me anyway."

"Anything I can do to help?"

"With Jessica or with this paper fest?" He waved his hand over his desk.

"Either one. I'm here to protect and serve."

Nick liked the way Eileen had fit in so easily in the detectives' room. All the guys seemed to like her.

"Eileen," Bill Fagan shouted from his desk in the far corner. "Phone call for you. Line three."

"Here." Nick stood up. "Take it at my desk. I was just about to head downstairs to the soda machine anyway. Can I bring you anything to wash down your coffee?"

"No, thanks," she said with a grin as she picked up the phone receiver.

When Nick returned, Eileen was no longer on the phone, but she was still sitting behind his desk. Her face was pasty white.

"What's wrong, Eileen? You should have recovered from Dub's coffee by now."

"Sorry, Nick. Bad news. My father's heart condition is worse."

"Oh, Eileen, I'm so sorry," he said, regretting his joke.

"They're going to try a bypass," she explained. "I hate that he's all alone. I really have to be there when he has surgery."

"Of course you should be with him," Nick agreed. "How soon are you leaving?"

"I haven't called the airport yet, but I guess I'll take the next available flight. I'm going to have to rush. As it is, I'll be lucky to get there before they take him in. I don't know how long I'll be gone."

"Do you want me to drive you to the airport?"

"No, thanks. I'll call Buddy."

Nick gave her a friendly hug and walked her to the door. "I hope your dad gets better real soon."

She smiled, but her eyes shone with tears. "What are you going to do about our investigation?"

"Don't give it another thought. You just take care of your dad."

"I guess I'd better break it to the chief."

As Eileen disappeared into Chief Wallace's office Nick sighed and leaned disgustedly against the gray-green wall. *This Verona Springs case must be jinxed,* he thought. *It started off bad enough with no clues and no real suspects. Then I screwed up my first attempt to fit in at the club. And now no partner. Without a partner I'll never get access to the sections of the club I need to see.*

Who could take Eileen's place? The only other woman detective in the office was old enough to be his mother. He could take one of the officers from another department, he supposed. Maybe Officer Layne Hickman from traffic, but he hated to suggest her. She'd been chasing him for two years, and he didn't want to give her any encouragement. And then there was Sergeant Betsy Craig—young enough, safe enough, but with her foghorn voice and barroom manners, he knew the country club setting would be too much of a stretch for her acting abilities.

He'd gone through the station's whole roster by the time Chief Wallace called him to his office. *Maybe I could take Jessica,* he thought, immediately wiping that idea from his mind. *The chief would never go for it. Besides, she's not even speaking to me.*

"You owe me, Tom Watts. You owe me big time!" Dana muttered under her breath as she stomped up the sidewalk to the small off-campus house where she lived with three other students. "You broke our date last Sunday and now you positively ruin our date today. You promised! Today was supposed to be you and me. *My* day. How dare you break your promise. How could you do this to me?"

Dana slammed the front door so hard, Felicity leaped from the couch in surprise. "What are you doing here?" she asked, clicking the remote to stop the videotape she'd been watching.

"I live here!" Dana shouted.

"I thought you and Tom were spending the whole day at that ritzy country club."

"We were supposed to, but . . ." Dana jerked the purple hat off her head and drop-kicked it across the room.

"Oh no. Tom broke the date again?"

"No. He didn't exactly *break* it. We went to the country club, all right. We were so close, I could hear the quartet playing in the distance— Mozart. You know how I adore Mozart. Then you-know-who showed up and ruined everything."

"Elizabeth?"

217

"None other than the news queen herself. She must have known we were going to be there. How am I supposed to keep Tom's mind off her when she follows us everywhere we go?"

"What'd he do?"

"Just stared at her like a big ol' hound dog looking at a pork chop. Then Elizabeth chased some old Mexican dude into the garden maze, and her new boyfriend went after them, and then Tom tried to—"

"Dana, you aren't making a bit of sense." Felicity led her over to the couch and forced her to sit down.

"I'm too mad to make sense," Dana said. "The whole day was ruined. Even after Elizabeth left, Tom wouldn't forget about her. He dragged me out to the parking lot like we were trying out for the track team. I practically begged him to stay at the club so we could hear the quartet, but no. He had to hightail it back to campus. And do you know what he said?"

Felicity sat on the edge of the coffee table and took Dana's hand. "What?"

"He said, 'Dana, I have work to do. I think that's a little more important than high tea and Mozart.'" She pulled her hand free of Felicity's and slammed it against the back of the couch. The dust that puffed out only made her angrier. She hit it again.

"Listen, Dana, if he doesn't want to be with

218

you, then maybe he's not the right guy for you."

"I *know* he wants to be with me." She got up from the dusty couch and began to pace back and forth in front of the TV. "He may not know it yet, but he will eventually."

"Well, they say all's fair in love and war," Felicity said, settling back into her place on the couch.

"You're right. And this is both. I'm in love with Tom and, as of now, I'm at war with Elizabeth Wakefield. I'm going to do whatever it takes to keep her away from Tom—no matter how drastic."

"I need someone tomorrow, Chief," Nick pleaded. "We can't be wasting any more time on this case. It's already been over a week since the murder."

"I don't know what we can do on such short notice." The chief scratched his chin thoughtfully. "What about that pretty little girlfriend of yours? She seems like the type that wouldn't be averse to a little playacting. Think you could convince her to take advantage of a fancy night out at the city's expense?"

Nick's finger flew to his ear. *Am I hearing right?* he wondered, swallowing back his surprise. Seeming too eager might jinx the good news. "I thought you were opposed to using civilians on a case, Chief."

"Obviously I don't want them around when the bullets start flying," the chief admitted, "but this assignment should be OK. Jessica won't be in any danger at a country club. Of course, there will be limits to what she can know and what she can do. We'll have to use her more or less as window dressing, but I think she'd do a fine job. And it's not like other men's wives and girlfriends haven't helped out on occasion." He leaned back in his chair. "Did I ever tell you about the time I got the bright idea to take my wife, Carol, on a stakeout? I'd just started on the force. . . ." He shook his hands in front of himself as if he were erasing a blackboard. "Oh, but that's another story. Come to think of it, it didn't work out very well, but we're running out of options here. If you don't think your girlfriend will want to do it, we'll just have to radio over to homicide and see if they have someone else who's suitable."

"I think Jessica would be willing to help out, sir," Nick said with as serious an expression as he could manage.

"Don't worry, Nick. As long as you watch out for her, she'll be fine."

"It's the bad guys who'll have to watch out once Jessica's on the job."

The chief laughed. "I thought so," he said. "Nick, that woman seems drawn to excitement like an ant to a picnic. I'll bet she's not scared of anything. Why don't you go on and call her and see what she says."

"Thank you, sir. I'll call her right now."

For all the good it'll do me, Nick thought as he walked back to his desk. *I've been calling since Friday night, and she hasn't spoken to me once. But if I can somehow get* this *message to her, she'll have to forgive me.*

Jessica plowed through the door into the police station, not even pausing to say hello to the usual faces that greeted her.

With her head down and her heels clicking against the hard tile floor, she charged down the hallway with her box of keepsakes. It seemed pathetic—all her time with Nick condensed into one single, lousy cardboard box. Angry tears stung her eyes, but she didn't let them fall. She wouldn't give Nick the satisfaction of letting him know how much he'd hurt her.

"Hey, Dressy Jessie!" Dub bellowed as Jessica burst into the detectives' room, but Jessica ignored him and marched straight to Nick's desk. He was on the phone, leaving a very tender message to someone—evidently his new partner!

"I love you," he purred disgustingly. "Please come down to the station as soon as you get this message." When he glanced up, he quickly dropped the phone.

Jessica's blood boiled. She'd caught him in the

act once again! "De-*tec*-tive Fox," she snarled.

"Jessica! I was just calling—"

"I don't want to hear it, Nick. I'm way past caring about who you call."

"I was calling *you*—for the ninety-ninth time."

"Well, you don't have to worry about calling me the *hundredth* time. Don't *ever* call me again. It's over between us, Nick."

Nick's green eyes widened. "If this is about Friday night—"

"Nick!" she shouted. She hadn't come here to listen. She wanted to say what she'd come to say and get it over with. Besides, if Nick looked at her with those emerald eyes and promised . . .

No—I can't let myself be talked out of this!

"Friday night is only *part* of it," she continued. "Of course I'm mad that you took that . . . that woman on a date, but our problem goes a lot deeper than your cheating."

"Whooo!" someone hooted from a nearby desk.

Jessica realized suddenly that she was drawing an audience, but at this point she didn't care. "You are *slime*, Nick Fox!"

"You go, girl," someone else shouted. "Let him have it!"

"You clearly have no respect for me. You don't care about my feelings. You don't want to share your life with me. I don't even think you want me around. You say you love me, but you don't really

222

know what love is. When you love someone, you care about their dreams and their hopes and—"

"Jessica, I think you should listen to me for a moment."

"No! I'm not *ever* listening to you again. You'd just lie anyway. I'm cutting you out of my life forever. And I hope you know what you've thrown away. I hope you regret it the rest of your life!"

"Jess, do you want me to give up my job?"

"You can keep your stinking job and your sexy partner, *and* you can keep all this junk too. Because I sure don't want it." She turned the box upside down and dumped all her ex-treasures across Nick's already cluttered desk. Two file folders slid off the desk, and papers fanned out like cards from a magician's hands. Nick was showered with dried flower petals like confetti. A teddy bear bounced off his chest and hit the floor. "I hope every single piece gives you a wonderful memory—a memory that you've *ruined!*" Jessica screamed, finishing her tirade. "Enjoy!"

The detectives who'd gathered to watch the fireworks hooted and applauded at her finale. Jessica spun on her heel and performed an exaggerated bow. Then she stalked toward the door.

"OK, Jess, you win."

She froze in her tracks but didn't turn around. As much as she loved hearing those words, she wouldn't be shaken from her conviction.

223

"You can help me out with my next undercover operation."

A shiver went up her spine as she spun around to face him. "*What* did you say?"

"I said you can help me. You can come with me. We'll be partners, just like you wanted. But you're going to have to start speaking to me again in a normal tone of voice if you want to get filled in on the details of our case."

Our case? It sounded too good to be true. She tilted her head to one side and gave him a skeptical look.

"Honest. In fact, it's already been approved. Ask the chief if you don't believe me."

Jessica glanced back to where Chief Wallace leaned against the open doorframe. In response to Jessica's questioning expression, the chief nodded.

Jessica's face exploded into a smile so big, it made her jaws ache. "Oh, Nick!" she cried, rushing around the desk and jumping into his lap. The momentum sent Nick's desk chair rolling backward off the plastic mat and into the wall.

"Well," Nick said calmly, his eyes dancing with amusement. "That was exciting."

"That was nothing compared to what our life will be like when we're partners."

"That's what I'm afraid of."

"You're the best boyfriend in the whole world!" she cried. "Did you know that?"

He brushed a strand of silky hair from her face

224

and tucked it behind her ear. "I know."

"And? What are you supposed to say next?"

"And?" He scratched his head in mock bewilderment. "And. . . I wonder what on earth I'm getting myself into."

"No, you're supposed to say . . ."

"And you're the best girlfriend in the world." His perfect teeth gleamed in a broad smile. "You are, Jess—the very best."

Jessica smothered his face with kisses, totally ignoring the hoots and cheers of the police officers who'd gathered around Nick's desk. From here on out, her life was going to be one moment of glorious excitement after another.

After running into Tom, Elizabeth couldn't get away from the club fast enough. Her hands were shaking, and her knees were so rubbery, she couldn't trust herself to drive.

"Here, Scott, would you mind?" She hastily handed him her keys. "I need to look over these brochures about the club and make a few notes. I'd rather to do it now while it's fresh in my mind."

"Sure." He took the keys from her hand, letting his own hand linger in hers a little longer than necessary.

"Thanks." She hurried around to the passenger side of the Jeep. *Fresh in my mind*, she thought. *What a laugh. The only thing fresh in my mind is the expression on Tom's face when he told me off. Why does he still have the power to churn up my insides like this?*

She spread a couple of club brochures in her lap and held a third in front of her face, but the words blurred into gray streaks. *I am not going to cry. I am absolutely, positively not going to cry.*

Think of the story, she told herself. *The story, always the story.* The chant worked. She was able to push thoughts of Tom aside long enough to return to the real matter at hand. Mr. Mendoza had been about to tell her something—and would have, if Tom hadn't spoiled everything. As quickly as she'd pushed Tom out of her mind, he popped back in. *Does he know about the murder? Is that why he was at the club?*

She felt like a cartoon character she'd seen once who had a little devil on one shoulder and a little angel on the other—both were whispering opposite ideas into her ears. But here the little shoulder-perched figures were both Elizabeth Wakefields—Old Elizabeth and New Elizabeth. Old Elizabeth was whispering, *"You don't want to compete with Tom. Think about how close you were. Remember all the dreams and hopes you once shared. Think about how well you worked together."*

But tiny New Elizabeth was saying, *"Go for it. Don't let him scoop your story. You found it. He doesn't care about you or your feelings, so why should you care about him?"*

Elizabeth's mind reeled with confusion. She didn't want to be in direct rivalry with Tom. It would be way too painful. Maybe for both of them.

Suddenly Scott's voice broke through the haze of her thoughts. "That was a cute girl Tom was with. Do you know who she was?"

"Yes, she's an absolute doll," Elizabeth growled, not pleased by the cattiness in her own voice but not willing to take it back either. "Her name is Dana Upshaw, if you're interested."

"Does she work at WSVU?"

"Hardly!"

Scott shrugged. "I just wondered. She looks familiar. I was almost positive that's where I'd seen her. Oh, well. Maybe I saw her there visiting Tom or something."

Elizabeth looked out the window at the blurred scenery. Her hands stayed clenched in her lap, but mentally she flicked the Old Elizabeth figure off her shoulder. *Why should I care what Tom Watts does? Tom is out of the picture. He is nothing more to me than a rival for a story. And like any rival, I'm going to smash him. He can't scoop my story. I won't let him. I know how he works. I know all his tricks and techniques.*

"He knows yours too," Old Elizabeth whispered, climbing back on her shoulder. This time Elizabeth literally laid her hand on her shoulder as if to brush the pest away.

Oh, I still have a few tricks up my sleeve, but if those don't work, then I'll simply have to come up with new ones, she thought. *I'm after you, Watts, with all guns blazing. This is my story, and you can't have it.*

"Elizabeth, are you all right? You've been awfully quiet since we left the club."

"Hmmm? Oh yes, I'm going to be fine," she assured him distractedly.

"Well, here we are back at SVU. Where to? The dorm, the library, or straight to the office?"

"I think the office. But drive down Maple past the television station, would you?"

Scott gave her a puzzled look but made the turn. "Do you think you'll be able to interview that gardener?"

"Huh? Oh, I'm going to interview him, of course. I think it might be better to find out where he lives and try to contact him away from the club." Elizabeth's eyes scanned the parking lot behind WSVU. Sure enough, Tom's car was already there. "Hurry up, Scott," she said. "Let's get back to the *Gazette* before we lose all these ideas."

As Scott brought the Jeep to a stop in front of the *Gazette* office he reached over and took Elizabeth's hand.

She yanked it away and glared at him but immediately regretted her rudeness. *He's only trying to comfort me,* she told herself. *Just because I'm hurt and angry at Tom, I shouldn't take it out on Scott.*

Scott didn't seem to take offense. He placed his hand gently on her shoulder. When she turned slightly to face him, he leaned across the space between their two seats and pulled her forward until her face met his. "Stop it!" she cried, but her words came out all muffled as he mashed his mouth against hers. She pried herself from his grasp and backed against the door until she felt the armrest jab her in the back. "What do think you're doing?"

"I'm just trying to stay in character," he replied casually. "We have to pose as a couple, remember?"

"Not in the car, we don't!" Elizabeth snarled as she fumbled for the door latch, jumped out of the Jeep, and wiped the offending kiss from her lips.

Will Jessica be able to stay undercover when she's surrounded by friends—not to mention her own twin sister? Find out in Sweet Valley University #34, SPY GIRL.